Tempt Me

Also By J. Kenner

The Stark Trilogy:
Release Me
Claim Me
Complete Me
Anchor Me

Stark Ever After:
Take Me
Have Me
Play My Game
Seduce Me
Unwrap Me
Deepest Kiss
Entice Me
Hold Me

Stark International
Steele Trilogy:
Say My Name
On My Knees
Under My Skin
Steal My Heart (short story - free download)
Take My Dare (novella)

Jamie & Ryan Novellas:
Tame Me
Tempt Me

Dallas & Jane (S.I.N. Trilogy):
Dirtiest Secret
Hot Mess
Sweetest Taboo

Most Wanted:
Wanted
Heated
Ignited

Tempt Me
A Stark International Novella

By J. Kenner

EVIL EYE
CONCEPTS

Tempt Me
A Stark International Novella
By J. Kenner

Published by Evil Eye Concepts, Incorporated

ISBN: 978-1-945920-09-7

Sign up for the 1001 Dark Nights Newsletter
and be entered to win a Tiffany Lock necklace.

There's a contest every quarter!

Go to www.1001DarkNights.com to subscribe.

As a bonus, all subscribers will receive a free
1001 Dark Nights story
The First Night
by Lexi Blake and M.J. Rose

Chapter One

More.

The word pounds into my head, beating a sensual rhythm in my blood.

More, yes. Please, please, more.

I'm neither awake nor asleep. Instead, I'm floating on a cloud somewhere above a horizon of dreams. I feel alive. I feel on fire.

I feel wildly, incredibly, insanely turned on.

Mostly, I feel loved. Cherished.

Arousal tugs at me, pulling me into consciousness. Into a place where I'm aware of the reason for the fire that rips through my body, igniting my skin and settling between my legs, making me achy and needy.

His lips. His hands.

They are roaming over me, strong and sure. Each caress like a tongue of flame. Each kiss a cool oasis, keeping me from melting under the heat that he is igniting inside me.

I know this touch, of course. This man.

Ryan Hunter.

I sigh, simply from the pleasure of his name in my mind. Hunter. *My Hunter.*

Before Hunter, I'd been with a lot of guys. Like, a *lot* of guys.

Once upon a time, that's something I took as a point of pride. That Jamie Archer could fuck around with the best of them, without ever letting anyone get too close. Because if you let them get too close, you could end up getting hurt.

But then Hunter came along and he broke through my defenses. *All* of my defenses.

He tamed me, and now he's always with me. In my heart. In my head.

Even now—with my eyes still closed, half-in and half-out of sleep—I can picture him. The thick, chestnut-colored hair that he wears short, but with just enough length that I can run my fingers through it. Fathomless blue eyes that see me so intimately. A long, lean body that he uses expertly—in bed and out of it.

He is so clear in my mind, and yet it's not enough. I want to actually see him. The humor and heat in his eyes. The way his lips twitch when he watches me, as if he can't decide if he wants to kiss me or devour me. The tightness of his jaw as he fights desire, holding back his own pleasure until he's made me explode again and again and again.

"Ryan," I murmur as I start to open my eyes, unable to wait a moment longer.

"No." The word is simple, yet firm. Full of the command that comes so naturally to him. And though I whimper, I acquiesce obediently. "Good girl." His voice washes over me like a warm caress, and I bite my lip, forcing myself to stay quiet.

"I want you lost in fantasy," he continues. "I want to watch your body move under my hand, not knowing where the next touch will be. Not knowing if I'm going to kiss your breast or spank your ass."

He does neither. In fact, his hands barely move at all. Instead, he simply grips my hips, his hands perfectly still. Only his thumbs move—a gentle back and forth caress that has hardly any more substance than a butterfly beating its wings, but to me is so intense that I can feel the thread of that contact all the way to my clit. I'm hot and wet and needy, and I writhe beneath him, silently begging for a more substantial touch.

He doesn't disappoint, and I cry out in both surprise and pleasure as his fingers pinch my nipples. Then moan when he crushes my mouth with a bruising kiss.

He runs his hands over me, his touch hard. Possessive. He palms my breasts, squeezing just enough that I arch up, wanting more. Wanting his mouth on my tit. Wanting him to suck. To tease.

But he leaves me wanting and instead draws his hands down. Not feather light this time, but with heat and pressure so that he leaves a trail of red hot fire down my body. So that when his hands stop at the juncture of my pelvis and my thighs, I cry out, "Please, Hunter, oh, fuck, please."

I can practically feel the heat of his skin on my cunt, and yet he doesn't move. Instead, he shifts his position and I feel the mattress dip, and then the warmth of his breath at my ear.

"I want all that," he whispers as he shifts his thumb just enough so that I feel it graze along the soft skin just above my clit. "Mouth. Breasts. Ass. Pain. Pleasure. And everything in between."

His thumb dips inside me, and I arch up, willing him to go deeper. To fill me.

But he's still teasing me, and instead of thrusting his fingers deep inside me, he withdraws them, forcing me to bite my lip simply to keep from whimpering.

"In other words, kitten," he murmurs as his thumb traces lazy circles around my clit, "I want you at my mercy."

"I am." My words are a gasp. "You know I am." The bed shifts again as I speak, and my skin feels cool as he removes his warm hands from my body. For a moment, panic rushes through me, and I fear that he's playing a game. That he's going to leave me here, naked and alone, lost with my thoughts of his touch, my skin flushing as I anticipate his return. As I fight the urge to touch myself when all I want is his hands on me and his cock deep inside me.

"Hunter." His name is a plea, and I reach out blindly, grasping for him.

"Shhh," he says, and the soft brush of his fingertip over my lips soothes me. "Wait," he says, as the finger moves lower and lower until finally I feel both hands on my hips, and he strokes them down along my outer thigh.

A pounding, liquid heat pools between my legs. I'm beyond aroused—I'm desperate. Wanton. And I move my hips in a silent demand that goes sadly, frustratingly unfulfilled.

"Christ, that's beautiful," he says as his hands reach my ankles and he slowly—so painfully slowly—spreads my legs. "You're so wet, you glisten. You're ripe, baby, so ripe I think I have to taste you."

The words have barely passed his lips when his mouth brushes my inner thigh and he begins to kiss me, higher and higher as his fingers trail along, lightly stroking the opposite thigh. I whimper and writhe, but then the intensity of his touch increases and instead of light strokes to my tender skin, his strong hands are holding me down. I'm immobile, trapped in place, my legs spread so wide it's almost painful, and I'm completely open to him. Completely exposed.

His tongue grazes the soft skin at the top of my thigh and I shudder. I try to squirm, but he's holding me tight. I hear someone begging and realize it's me. A soft "please, please, oh please, yes, please" escaping my lips, barely a murmur, and so much more like a prayer.

Finally, his mouth closes over my sex and he sucks and teases, playing with my overly sensitive clit as I try to move—to relieve some of this astounding, amazing, incredible assault. But I can't, and I can only endure it as a storm builds inside me, brought on by a pleasure so intense that it crosses over into pain.

And then, just as my body starts to quake with sweet release, he pulls back, gently stroking me, his tongue dipping inside me, thrusting hard, and I cry out, because I want more. I want to be filled completely. I want to feel my body stretching, welcoming him. I want him to own me. To use me. I want to break apart under the power that is this man I love.

"Hunter," I cry out, and as he lifts his hands to let me move, I piston my hips, fucking his tongue as he slides his hands up and cups my breasts, his thumbs teasing my nipples. "Please," I beg, because at this point I am officially desperate. "Please," I repeat as my eyes flutter open. "I want to feel you inside me."

He lifts his head, his expression a mix of passion and playfulness, then kisses his way up my body with slow, lingering caresses designed to drive me even wilder than I already am.

"Ryan—" But he silences me with a long kiss, so deep and intimate and claiming that it feels like fucking.

"Shhh," he murmurs, his mouth brushing mine. Tasting mine. Teasing my lips. Tracing a path along my jaw as his fingers dip deep inside me. "You're so wet," he says as I lose my mind and grind against him. I want him. I want everything. And I'm both frustrated that he isn't yet giving it to me, and deliciously, wildly, insanely turned on by the way he's extending this unimaginable pleasure into an infinite, crazed delight.

"I don't want to stop," he admits. "I want to keep teasing you. I like it when you beg, kitten. I like hearing how much you want me. Tell me again, baby. Tell me what you want."

"You." My voice is cracked, as shattered as my body. "I want you inside me. I want you to come inside me."

"Christ, Jamie," he says, his voice sharp and urgent. "I can't take it any longer. Turn over, kitten. On your knees for me."

I comply eagerly. Right then I'd hang from the damn chandelier if he asked me to, even though we don't even have a chandelier. I just want him. Want to please him. Want to feel him.

"Beautiful," he murmurs once I'm on my knees, my head on the pillow and my elbows on the bed. His hand smacks my ass lightly, and I groan, squeezing my legs together to fight the growing sense of pressure in my cunt. I'm so fucking turned on right now that another touch could send me spiraling over the edge, and that's not what I want. Not yet.

No, what I want is to feel him inside me. I want that connection, that most intimate union, and when I finally feel his cock at my opening, my entire body rejoices. *This.* This is what I want. This man, one with me.

"Yes," I beg. "Now, Ryan. *Now.*"

I'm beyond wet, and when he grips my hips and thrusts forward, his cock fills me. He stays still for a moment, our bodies joined, then pulls out before slamming back into me again and again and again. Wilder and faster, in a rhythm that has me gasping, my hips moving in time with his thrusts so as to make it deeper.

"I adore you," he murmurs. "Christ, you feel good."

"Yes," I murmur, because my mind can't come up with any more words. "More."

His laugh is low and throaty, and he slips one hand off my hip then slides it around to tease my clit. He's thrusting slower now, and when he takes his other hand from my hip, I bite my lower lip, unsure what he's up to. But then I feel his fingertip stroking from my vagina to my ass, and my body shakes under the onslaught of my coming orgasm, my cunt tightening around his rock-hard cock.

"That's it, baby. I want to make you crazy."

I'm desperately wet, and when he teases my anus with his thumb, it's wet and slick with my own desire. Then he presses it inside me, slowly at first, and then faster as I relax, so that his finger fucks my ass as his cock pumps harder and harder, the tempo increasing again until I am reduced to little more than sensation and need and greedy lust.

His fingertip teases my clit as he thrusts his finger and his cock harder and harder, and I piston my hips, wanting this to continue forever almost as much as I want to explode right this very moment. I want to shatter.

I want it to never be over.

I want Hunter.

"Ryan," I beg. "God, Ryan, please."

And then, without warning, my muscles clench tight around him, my whole body shot through with electricity, my core milking him as he cries out too as his body explodes inside of me, and I'm twisting and moaning, wanting both to escape from this onslaught of sensation and to experience it fully. I'm lost in a dance of colors so wild, so incredible, so intensely beautiful, that I'm certain this must be what heaven looks like. At least, it's the heaven that Hunter and I made together.

Slowly, I come back to my senses, and realize that I'm biting down hard on the pillow, as if that was my tether to the earth.

Ryan has moved beside me, and now he cradles me against the warmth of his body.

"I think you broke me," I murmur, and though I can't hear his responding laugh, I feel the rumble in his chest.

"I hope it was worth it."

I shift so that I'm facing him, our legs intertwined, his semi-erect cock brushing against my sensitive pussy. "Very," I say, then reach down and gently stroke him.

I see a flare of heat in his eyes and his cock twitches with obvious interest. But while the body is obviously willing, the man shakes his head, and I still my hand. "That was your wake-up call. Good morning," he says, then kisses my nose.

"If that was a wake-up call, I'm giving up my alarm clock and relying on you every day."

"I wouldn't protest," he says. And though he'd shaken his head just a moment before, he reaches down and slides my hand over his cock, obviously ordering me to start stroking him again.

I lift a brow, amused. "Or maybe we should always set an alarm. That way we remember to wake up and fuck."

"I don't need a reminder to remember to make love to you."

I grin. "No?"

"Never."

I sigh, knowing that's the truth.

Ryan and I have been together for a couple of years now, and I've never felt happier or more loved. He's truly my knight. A man who, quite literally, rescued me when I tried to run away. From him. From a life that really wasn't working out the way I wanted or had imagined.

Now, though, I have him, and every day feels like a gift. He's loyal, protective, and sexy as hell. And I've gone from being a girl who went through men as if they were candy—sweet, delicious, but not something good for you—to being a woman who knows that Ryan is the best thing that ever happened to me. He loves me—faults and bad choices and all.

And that's a damn nice feeling.

Lord knows he's seen me at my worst. He's the Security Chief at Stark International, and his boss and best friend is Damien Stark, the multi-billionaire who happens to be my best friend's husband. So Ryan has had a bird's-eye view of so many of my bad choices. He's seen me drunk. He's seen me dumped. He's seen a parade of bad choices pass in front of me, and he knew damn well they were passing through my bed.

And yet all that time, he'd wanted me. Not as a fast fuck, but as something more. And he'd gone after me with singular determination.

I'd been terrified at first.

Now, I don't know how I could survive without him beside me.

Hell, he loves me so much that he wants to marry me—and that's a nice feeling, too. But it's tainted by a black thread of fear. Because while I'm happy with the thought of spending the rest of my life with Ryan, the idea of formalizing it with marriage vows makes me twitchy.

It's making me twitchy now, just thinking about it. And so, like I often do, I brush the thought from my head and roll over to curl up closer to him. I breathe in his scent and sigh, because he smells like home. "I like having days off," I murmur. "I'd forgotten how much I enjoyed it when my weekends were free." I've recently landed a job as a weekend anchor for a local news affiliate. It's a great gig, but I do miss these lazy Sundays.

"Well, we can't be too lazy. We're meeting Nikki and Damien over at Jackson and Sylvia's place. And," he adds, glancing down at his now steel-hard erection that I'm stroking, "I think we're going to be late as it is."

"Phhht." I wave my other hand as if brushing away his words. "They have a house. They have kids. They're not going anywhere." I give his shoulder a shove, so that I push him onto his back as I release his cock. In the same movement, I straddle him, nice and low on the hips. Then I start to move, wiggling my ass just a little as I lean forward, sliding my hands slowly up his rock-hard abs, then higher and higher until I'm pretty much doing yoga on the man, as my torso is flat against his, while my legs are still spread across him, and the head of his cock teases my rear.

And I'm wet—so wet and so turned on all over again. I shimmy a bit, wanting to feel the hair above his cock rough against my sensitive clit. And his cock—oh, yes—I want that bad. I lift my hips in slow, easy movements so that his shaft slides along the crack of my rear.

I meet his eyes—and I see both amusement and a wild heat reflected back at me. "No more teasing," he says. "Slide that beautiful pussy down and fuck me."

"Yes, sir," I say, then do exactly as he says, drawing him in so slowly we both are going crazy with need. And then, when he's deep inside me, we rock together in slow, sensual motions.

"Kiss me," he says, and I close my mouth over his, losing myself in the sensation of being body on body like this, so close I can't tell if the heartbeat I'm feeling belongs to Ryan or me.

We move slowly at first, but there's no holding back, and soon our motions are frenzied. Soon, he's exploding inside me.

Soon, I shatter in his arms.

"Oh, baby," he murmurs when we're sane again and he's looking at my face with eyes filled with love. "You are so beautiful."

I bend and kiss him—my heart overflowing. And I can't help but think how different it is with Ryan than the men I'd been with before. Before, when a guy called me beautiful, I'd mentally cringed, at least a little.

Because the truth is, I *am* beautiful. It's not an ego thing— it's just an empirical fact. It's useful, and I've definitely traded on it. But it's not who I am. Not the heart of me. And in my life BR—Before Ryan—whenever a guy called me beautiful, I never knew if he cared about me, or if he was just happy to have a pretty piece of ass.

With Ryan, I know without a doubt that he loves me. And the beauty he sees in me is more than what a camera sees.

He sees the whole woman. A lover, a friend. He sees a girl he can laugh with. That he can talk to. A woman to spend long, lazy nights with. A woman with hopes and dreams and fears and doubts.

He sees me. *Jamie Archer.* And that's a really nice feeling.

"I love you," I say, those little words just spilling out of me. "You're the best thing that ever happened to me."

The moment I say the words, though, I regret them. Not because they aren't true—they are. But because I can see the response on Ryan's face, though he knows enough not to say the words out loud.

If that's true, then why won't you marry me?

God knows he understands marriage scares me. And, thankfully, he's patient.

But the day will come when understanding won't be enough and when his patience has worn thin.

He'll want an answer. A solid yes or a solid no.

And what the hell am I going to do then?

Chapter Two

"Again, Miss Jamie! Again!"

"Again?" I ask, as I come around the swing so that I can look into Ronnie's big blue eyes, so wide and innocent and pleading. "Aren't you tired? Wouldn't you rather play with your brother in the sandbox?"

Her lips purse as she tilts her head sideways. She's almost six, and she takes every question very seriously. "No," she says after a moment of deep thought. "Wanna swing more. Wanna go higher. Please, Miss Jamie. Please, please, pleeeeeeeeeeeeese?"

As the final plea is still ringing in the air, my BFF and Ronnie's aunt—Nikki Stark—walks by carrying two paper plates. One with a hamburger patty, a few cubes of cheese, and four apple slices. The other with a burger piled so high with cheese and lettuce and tomatoes it makes my mouth water. "You may as well give in," Nikki says to me. "The kid's relentless."

"I am," Ronnie says eagerly. "I'm rent-less! So push, Miss Jamie. Push me higher. Please, please, pretty please."

I catch Nikki's eye just long enough to see her smirk before she continues on toward the sandbox, where Ronnie's little brother, Jeffery, is building a castle with the kids' nanny, Stella. Although *building* is a bit of an exaggeration; he's still baby enough that Stella is doing most of the work, and Jeffery is mostly a destructive, sand-tossing force.

"Burgers are ready!" Sylvia, the kids' mother, calls to us from the rooftop patio of the amazing house that her husband, the world-renowned architect Jackson Steele, designed. "Ronnie, come get yours, and then you can play with Jeffery and Stella while Jamie takes a break. Otherwise, you're going to wear her out."

Ronnie nods obediently, but then she tilts her head up to me, her expression earnest. "Please?" This time, the word emerges as a whisper. "Just one time?"

"One push," I say, fighting a smile. "Then you go get your burger like your mom said."

She nods eagerly, black curls bouncing, and I move around to give her one big push. Then I surprise her with just one more, and she squeals and kicks her legs and cries out, "I'm flying! I'm flying!"

"You sure are, rug rat," I say. "And when you come down, you go get your burger, okay?"

"Yes, ma'am," she answers politely, but her legs are still kicking and she's still pushing toward the sky as I fall in step beside Nikki, who's back from delivering the meals to Stella and Jeffery.

We walk in silence for a few moments, but as we approach the house, Nikki slows. I match her pace until we end up at a standstill at the base of the outdoor staircase that leads up to the roof.

I point up to where Syl and the men are waiting for us. "Are we—?"

"In a minute." Nikki cocks her head, then crosses her arms over her chest. "Well?"

I shake my head, completely baffled.

"Don't even," Nikki says. "I know you too well. Something's up." Her eyes narrow. "Did Ryan quit hinting around and finally ask you to marry him?"

"What? No." I frown. "Why do you think so?"

"Because you're acting like you have every time he's brought up the subject."

"I am not," I say, but I'm speaking automatically, and when I actually think about it, I have to agree that she's right.

"Oh, please," Nikki says, then proceeds to voice what I'm thinking. "You practically jumped at the chance to push Ronnie on the swings."

"I adore Ronnie," I say truthfully.

"*And*," Nikki continues, "instead of dragging Ryan with you like you usually do, you suggested he go help Jackson at the grill."

"Ryan flips a mean burger," I say, despite the fact that it's a completely lame protest.

"And you grabbed a chair instead of claiming that double chaise lounge you always take. He noticed, you know."

I bite my lower lip. "Do you really think he did?"

She nods. "So what's going on?"

I drag my fingers through my hair. "Nothing intentional, I promise. I mean, I'm not trying to push him away if that's what you mean. I didn't even realize I was doing any of that. Not until after you said, and—"

"And I'm right. Yay me. But *why*? I mean, I get it if he asked you to marry him. Or, rather, I get why you'd be awkward around him. For the record, I don't get why you haven't jumped all over that."

"He hasn't brought it up since last time. Right before Damien's birthday." My voice is low, almost a whisper.

"Okay. Fine. But what happened today?"

I sigh. "I told him I love him. I told him that he's the best thing that ever happened to me."

Her eyes go wide. "You've never told him you love him?"

"Oh, sure. Of course, I have. But today—I don't know. It felt different. Like, I don't know…" I trail off with a shrug.

"Like maybe you actually could marry him?"

"Well," I say, "now that I think about it, yeah."

She blinks, and I have the feeling she's trying very hard to organize her thoughts so that she doesn't either laugh or call me a lunatic. "James," she finally says, using the nickname she'd given me ages ago. "I love you. But sometimes I really don't understand you."

I grimace. "Sometimes, *I* don't understand me."

Nikki looks at me but says nothing, so I just keep on talking. "It's just—I don't know. I never thought I could fall in love. I mean, you know me. All sex, no depth. At least until Ryan. And then when he and I got together, I was so scared that I'd lose myself if I became part of a couple. That it would be bliss—but that I'd subjugate my own ambition. I wouldn't go after my dreams because I'd already be living a dream."

"But you don't think that anymore," Nikki points out. "And Ryan hasn't held you back. You guys are great together *and* your career is doing amazing *and* Ryan's your biggest fan."

"He is," I say. "He really is."

"How's the present going, by the way?"

My smile is fast and genuine. "Really great, actually. But I'm going to need your help for a few of the shots later this week." We're talking about a Valentine's Day present for Ryan that I've been working on in my spare time—although with V-Day fast approaching, I need to get moving if I'm going to have it ready by next Saturday, when Ryan and I have impossible-to-get reservations at Bistro 85, the hottest new place in town.

Valentine's Day is actually just a few days away on Tuesday, but since Ryan has to work on the fourteenth, we're doing our celebration a few days after the rest of the world.

That's okay by me. I've never been one for following the rules.

"I'm happy to help," Nikki says. "But what do you need?"

"Just for you to operate the camera. I need some shots of me with the camera zooming in on my face as I talk. I can't zoom in and out when I shoot from a tripod."

My new weekend anchor gig is a great stepping stone, but my ambition is to be an on-air reporter covering the entertainment beat. And, after I've gained a following there, I want to host my own entertainment show.

Ryan knows all that, of course. He more than knows it—
he's an ardent champion. He's even gone so far as to arrange
meetings for me with network executives he's met through his
work. So far, nothing has popped, but that's not for lack of
support from the man I love. And so for Valentine's Day, I'm
making him a personalized newscast wherein his favorite
reporter—me—shares just how amazing he's been in the time
we've been together. Amazing in all sorts of ways, including a
few that are NC-17. But I'm only recruiting Nikki to help with
the PG-13 clips, wherein I tell him just why I'm so madly in
love with him.

Which brings me right back to the central question—if I
love him, and he loves me, why the hell am I running?

"I guess I'm afraid that marriage will mess it all up," I tell
Nikki, who doesn't seem at all surprised by my abrupt segue
back to the original topic. "That everything is going great now,
but that if we get married, we're going to tip the scales and the
universe is going to punish us."

"Do you really believe that?" she asks gently. "Did it mess
everything up for me and Damien? For Sylvia and Jackson?"

I lift a shoulder. She's right, of course. Both couples are
walking, talking proof that marriage doesn't screw anything up
where love is concerned. If anything, it strengthens it. But the
difference is that neither Nikki nor Syl were running from love
in the first place—they had their issues, and big ones—but they
were never afraid of love.

"I know," I say. "I do. But what if it all goes away? What if
I go all in, and then it all shatters under me?"

She takes my hand, her expression a little sad and a little
earnest. "Love's not supposed to be that scary, James."

"Yeah?" I pull my hand back and shove it in the pocket of
my jeans, then look down at the grass. "Then you're doing it
wrong. Because I think love's terrifying. Opening your heart
like that. Putting yourself on the line."

I suck in a breath and look up at her, and the thing is that
I get it—I really do understand what she's saying. But my heart

is refusing to follow where my head's already gone.

"Right now, everything is great," I continue, trying to put words to this maelstrom of fear and feelings. "Why can't we just stay this way? I mean, if I don't want to get married, why can't he understand and just keep going as is? For me?"

"But that goes both ways, doesn't it? If you're saying it won't change anything, then why can't you just say yes? For him."

I scowl at her. "I hate it when you're logical."

Her smile lights up her face, and in that brief instant, I see again why she won pageant after pageant back when her mother forced her to enter the damn things every fifteen minutes. "All I'm saying is Ryan's a great guy," she says. "And there's nothing wrong with him wanting you as his wife. Wanting a family."

"He already has me," I say stubbornly. But it's true. I think of the beautiful, silver collar he bought me when we first got serious. I wear it often, though not always. But even so, if that's not proof that he owns me completely, I don't know why a wedding band would make it more real.

"I know you better than anyone, James, and you know I love you. So trust me when I say this with your best interest at heart—don't let fear screw up the best thing you've got going for you."

I scowl. But I'm saved from answering by Sylvia's voice calling down from above to Ronnie. Once the little girl leaps from the swing, Sylvia's attention shifts to Nikki and me. "Are you two ever coming up?"

"Sorry," Nikki yells back. "On our way. Just think about it," she adds in a softer voice as we start up the stairs.

I don't bother answering, but her words seep inside me. The truth is, I know she's right. But fear is a funny thing. It gets under your skin. It disguises itself as reason. It's insidious and sneaky and it wants to win.

But here's the good news: I'm competitive as hell. And somehow, someway, I'm going to kick fear's ass.

Chapter Three

"No more," I say, as Ryan offers me a spoonful of chocolate ice cream. "I'm completely stuffed." It's no exaggeration. I'm practically comatose after a burger, a hot dog, approximately eight million potato chips, and some of Jackson's incredible coleslaw.

We've spent an entire lazy, wonderful day here with our friends. We'd started with a light brunch, then had this fabulous picnic-style dinner, and now I'm stretched out on the double chaise, just vegging out. Ryan is propped up beside me, our shared bowl of ice cream balanced on my stomach.

"You're sure?" He touches the tip of the spoon to my lower lip. I instinctively lick it, then sigh with pleasure at the cool, chocolatey sweetness.

"Mmm," I say. "I can't eat another bite."

"In that case..." He moves the spoon to his lips, his eyes locked on mine as he licks it clean—and I feel my body clenching simply from watching that amazing mouth and tongue. "Delicious," he says, and I know damn well he isn't talking about the ice cream.

I clear my throat, then shift. The first, because my mouth has gone dry and I need to regain the ability to form words. The second, because if I stay like this, with my body so hyperaware of the man beside me, I'm going to end up embarrassing myself in front of my friends. Right now, Jackson and Syl are down in the yard, while Nikki and Damien are standing at the rail looking out over the backyard toward the ocean. But I'm sure Syl and Jackson are on their way back. And any moment now, Nikki and Damien could turn around.

"Kiss me quick," I whisper, and he doesn't waste any time. His mouth closes over mine, cool and sweet, and I close my eyes, letting his touch sweep me away, emptying my mind of all my fears and doubts, and silencing that horrible voice that seems to yell the loudest when I'm the happiest.

"Funny," Damien says, his voice drifting toward us from across the patio, "I didn't realize it was already Valentine's Day."

I feel the heat rise in my cheeks as Ryan breaks the kiss. I open my eyes to see him wink at Damien. "Come on in," Ryan says. "The water's fine."

"Don't mind if I do," Damien says, and pulls Nikki to him with such ardent zeal that I hear her surprised little, "*oh*," from all the way across the patio. He claims her with a wild kiss, but I only see the first moment of connection, because Ryan takes me just as savagely, and I close my eyes and sink into the feel of him. A delicious warmth fills me. I'm desired. Loved.

Special.

And then, when I hear the sharp clearing of Jackson's throat, I feel as guilty as a teenager caught by her parents.

We break apart, laughing, and I see that Nikki and Damien have done the same.

"Honestly," Jackson says to Syl. "We leave the kids alone for just a few minutes..."

"Oh, I don't know." She hooks her arms around his neck. "I think they have the right idea."

He laughs and kisses her, and when they break apart we're all laughing together.

"I'm so glad you all came over today," Sylvia says as she takes Jackson's hand and pulls him over to sit on the end of the chaise that Ryan and I have claimed. "I was afraid we wouldn't be able to all get together before Jackson and I head off."

"I'm jealous," I admit. "Getting whisked away over Valentine's Day. And to Hawaii. Very, very jealous."

"Don't be too jealous," she says. "It's a ten-day work trip, after all." She leans forward, then says in a mock-whisper. "Of course, we'll probably sneak in some free time. Just don't tell my boss."

Sylvia's a project manager with Stark Real Estate Development, and she's in charge of a new resort that's going up on one of the Hawaiian islands. Designed by none other than Jackson, of course.

"I heard that," Damien says with a chuckle from where he still stands with Nikki at the rail. "Besides, your boss is going to have his hands full juggling meetings in Austin."

"Not too full," Nikki says. "I'm taking time off to come with you, after all. I expect at least one or two quality hours with my husband. Especially on Valentine's Day."

"I can probably squeeze out a minute or two for you," he says, then kisses her nose. "If you're very, very good."

I roll my eyes. "You realize you're all far too sappy. What's the point of Valentine's Day if you're sappy all year round?"

"Are you two doing it up big for Valentine's Day?" Syl asks, looking at me. I glance at Ryan, but he's looking away, as if he wants to avoid the question. Actually, maybe he does. After all, he has to work on Valentine's Day—something that I'm not particularly thrilled about since he runs the entire security division, and it seems to me that he should practice the manly art of delegating the crappy hours to someone else.

"Ryan has to work," I say, sticking my tongue out at Damien, who laughs. "So we're just going to have a late drink at home on Tuesday. But we'll have our own private Valentine's Day on the weekend. Fortunately, I only work Thursday and Friday this week. I have two weekends in a row completely off."

I sigh dramatically. "But on Tuesday I'll be all alone with

my thoughts. Maybe a racy romance novel. A bubble bath. But no man beside me." I prop myself up on my elbow and focus on Damien. "Such a shame my boyfriend works for such a slave driver."

Damien holds his hands up in surrender. "This one's not on me. The man's just too damn qualified. The system tests have to happen on Tuesday, and Ryan has to be there."

"What can I say?" Ryan adds. "I'm essential."

I hook my arm around his neck, then pull him to me for a quick kiss. "Yes," I say sincerely. "You are."

"Does anyone want more food? A refill on a drink?" Syl stands and heads over to the kitchen area, glancing at each of us in turn.

"I couldn't eat another bite." I flop back onto the chaise. "In fact, I'm not sure I can ever move again. I may have to just stay here forever. Right on this lounge chair." I turn my head so that I can see both Syl and Jackson. "You guys don't mind, do you? I don't take up that much room."

"No problem," Sylvia says, but Ryan stands and scoops me up into his arms.

"No way," he says. "You're not getting away from me that easily. In fact," he adds as I kick and squeal, "we should probably be going. I have plans for this woman tonight."

"Oh, you do?" I catch Nikki's eyes. She's smiling, but I see a hint of worry on her face, and realize it's from our earlier conversation.

"I do," he confirms. "And trust me, Jamie, you want privacy."

The others laugh, and we say our good-byes after Syl assures me that she doesn't need help cleaning up. Then Ryan carries me all the way down to his sleek 2005 Thunderbird convertible, which I think is one of the prettiest cars on the road.

The sun hangs low in the sky as I settle into the passenger seat, and Ryan eases the car out of the drive. As soon as we're heading down the hill toward the Pacific Coast Highway, he reaches over and takes my hand.

"Good day?"

"A great day," I say. And then, even though the words scared me just this morning, I shift in my seat to face him and say, "I love you."

He lifts my hand to his lips and kisses my fingers. "You have no idea how much I like hearing that."

My smile grows wide, and I sit back, content, as we head toward the ocean, vast and alight with so much evening color it looks like the backdrop of a movie set.

Nikki and Damien and Sylvia and Jackson are probably still on the patio. Still looking toward the west and seeing this very same view. I can picture both couples so clearly. Damien's arm around Nikki's shoulders. Jackson standing behind Sylvia, his arms possessive around her waist. They're all so blissfully happy. More than that, they fit together.

They fit the same way that Ryan and I fit.

I squeeze his hand, and he glances at me. "Hey, kitten."

"You say it like that, and you make me want to curl up and purr."

"Is that so? Well, tell me how I say it so I never stop."

I glance down at the floorboard, feeling suddenly awkward as I whisper, "You say it like I'm everything in the world to you."

"Oh, kitten, don't you know that you are?"

I nod, and then I say the only thing I can, because it's the absolute truth. "Yeah. I do."

He stops at a light and turns to me more fully. We're facing the sunset, but I don't think it's the vibrant light that has put that heat in his eyes. "Do you?" he asks. "Sometimes I wonder if you really understand how much I feel for you."

My heart twists in my chest, and right then I wish I could kick my own ass. Just the thought that I've hurt him—that he's doubted me for even a minute—makes me want to cry. I've been so wrapped up in my own fears, I never thought that he would begin to doubt.

"Ryan," I say, my throat thick with unshed tears. "I do know it. And I hope you know that I'm yours. Because I am. Completely."

I see the flicker of a smile on his lips. Then the light changes and he turns away, making a left turn onto the Coast Highway and heading for home. He'll keep driving until we hit Santa Monica and the 10, where we'll quit skirting the coastline and head inland toward home. Ryan has a small one-bedroom house here in Malibu, but for the past few months he's spent ninety percent of his time at my place in Studio City. It's closer to both our jobs, and it has the advantage of a second bedroom—the one that used to be Nikki's—that I use as both an office and an overflow closet.

Plus, I like being in my place. I'd almost given it up when I'd moved back to Texas not long ago. Ryan's the one who pulled me back to LA, but if I'd moved in with him and let my tenant keep the condo indefinitely, it would have felt like I lost a piece of me.

Maybe that's my problem. Maybe I'm looking at love as giving something up, instead of making something better.

It's an unpleasant thought, mostly because it feels so dead-on accurate. And it probably makes sense, too. My parents have always been madly, blissfully in love. So much so that I felt like a third wheel my entire life. Loved, yes. I was never neglected or abused or any of the horrors you hear about these days. But neither of my parents adored me as much as they adored each other. And they both sacrificed so much. My mother gave up law school. My father abandoned his dreams of painting. They didn't ask each other to do that—but they each walked away from things they loved because they wanted to give that extra time to each other.

I've always been terrified that I'd do the same. That love was so consuming it stole a piece of you.

But now I think of Ryan. I think of my friends, all so desperately, fully in love.

Mostly, I think that I've been wrong.

I settle back in my seat, feeling more content than I've been in weeks, and that's when I realize that we're no longer on the highway. Ryan has turned off, and is now maneuvering the lanes of a public parking area. I glance around to get my bearings and discover that we're in the parking lot next to the iconic Gladstone's restaurant. "You can't possibly be hungry," I say.

"Not the restaurant," he says as the attendant points him toward an empty slot. "I thought we'd take a walk and watch the sunset."

That sounds about as awesome as awesome gets, and soon enough my hand is in his and we're walking down the path to the sand. It's loose at first, and I slip a bit. Ryan catches me before I fall, then presses a kiss to my temple. When he pulls back, his eyes search mine, and I feel a catch in my chest, like I'm holding in a gasp. There's power in his eyes. In the way he's watching me. And I feel as though we've hit some sort of crossroads without either of us really knowing how we got here.

I expect him to say something. To give me an ultimatum. To tell me that I've been an idiot—basically, I expect him to lay out for me everything I've been thinking.

But he doesn't. He just holds me. Just looks at me.

And then he nods a bit, as if he's seen something in me that satisfies him. And then he takes my hand again and says, very simply, "Let's walk."

"Okay." I'm not sure if I'm relieved or frustrated. But I fall in step beside him, and we head down to the surf. The water in the Pacific is always cold, but it's colder in February, and we keep our shoes on and walk just out of reach of the incoming waves.

"I need to go to Boston," he says after we've walked for about five minutes in silence. I'd been looking to my right at the grand expanse of the Pacific and the sun now hanging like a vibrant ball, just inches above the horizon.

Now, I turn away from the cacophony of color that is

bleeding across the water, oranges and purples so rich they make my heart ache from the beauty of it. "For work? Or your mom?"

"Mom," he says. "Her sixtieth birthday is Friday. I thought I'd fly out on Thursday."

"Oh. Okay." I have no idea where this wave of melancholy has come from, but I smile my way through it.

"I'd rather you go with me," he says. "But I know you're working."

"Really?" I ask, and the sadness disappears, brushed aside by the certainty that he wants me there.

His brow furrows. "Jamie—I..."

His words have trailed off, and he's turned away from me, so that he's looking out at the sunset, too. The deep orange sun is now sitting on the horizon, and in my mind, I hear the sizzle as gallons upon gallons of seawater boil from contact with the fiery orb.

"Ryan?" I ask tentatively. "What were you going to say?"

He turns to me, and I see an unexpected vulnerability in his eyes. "You baffle me sometimes," he says. "How can you not know that I'd want you to go with me? Sixty years, and so much of that without my father. I want her to be with family. With me. With Moira. And the person who's most important to me at my side."

I swallow a knot of tears. Ryan's father died in the line of duty when his sister—who'd been a surprise and is much younger than Ryan—was only eight. Ryan became the man of the house, almost a father to Moira. And family is incredibly important to him.

"Do you really not understand how much you mean to me?" he continues. "Or are you just too stubborn to let yourself believe it?"

I open my mouth to answer him and taste the salt of those damn tears. "I don't know. I guess the bottom line is that you've fallen for a girl who's a complete basket case."

"Don't talk trash about the woman I love."

I smile at that, then slide into his arms and let him hold me tight. It feels so safe in his embrace. So *right*.

I release a long, slow breath. "I know you've been frustrated with me lately," I say carefully.

"With *you*? Not possible."

I can hear the humor in his voice, and I fight not to smirk.

"You couldn't be frustrating if you tried," he continues.

It's so ridiculous that I can't help but bark out a laugh. "And that's why I love you," I say sincerely. "You take me as I am."

"As you are is what I love."

It takes me a second to unwind that sentence in my head, but when I do I'm smiling. "That is *so* not grammatically correct," I say.

Ryan's lips barely curve, but the smile still reaches his eyes. "Maybe not. But it's heartfelt."

I don't answer. Instead, I take his hand as we continue walking along the sandy shore.

"My mother adores you," he says once the gray of twilight has settled around us.

"You mean she doesn't know what to make of me," I counter. In fact, his mom has only met me twice, but I've loved her from the first minute I met her. "She says that your dad would have called me Spitfire." I pretend to be affronted, but I know Ryan can hear the affection in my voice.

"He probably would have. And he'd have been right on the money," Ryan adds, and I hip-bump him. "I really want you there—"

"Ryan, don't. You know I have to work, and you're just going to make me feel bad. I mean, I'd love to see her, too." And the fact that he wants me there only makes the not going worse. The last thing I want is for him to rub it in.

"I was thinking maybe I should fly her out here instead. Do it up big. Get her a suite at a fancy hotel. Maybe arrange a full day for her and Moira at a spa. You, too, if you want. But if that's too much, at least you could get away for a dinner, couldn't you?"

"I—" I stop walking so that I can face him. "I could totally make a dinner work. But don't you want to go home for her birthday? Won't her friends want to celebrate, too?"

"It's up to her, but I think she'd like the trip. I've been wanting to do this for a while, but she always turns me down. But I think for sixty years, she'll agree. It's a big deal, after all."

"Yeah, it is. And you—"

"It's a big deal," he repeats softly. "I'd like you to be part of it."

My cheeks hurt and I realize my smile is stretched impossibly wide. "Okay. If she's in, so am I. I think it sounds great."

"Then that's the plan." He leans in and brushes a kiss to my temple, then whispers, "Thanks, Spitfire."

I playfully smack him as I back away. I don't get far, though, because he pulls me back, his arms going immediately to encircle my waist. We're pressed close together and I can feel his erection through his jeans. It's a moment that's both sweet and sexual, and right then I know that I have to have this man.

Not physically—well, not right now; I'm content to wait until we get home to strip him naked.

No, I want to *have* him. Physically, emotionally, *completely*.

And I really don't understand what's been holding me back.

"Do you remember that day in Vegas?" I ask. "When I was an idiot and left and you came after me?"

"I have a vague recollection."

"We looked over and there was a billboard for a Vegas wedding chapel. And you said something about how we could head on over there."

He stays quiet, but I feel the muscles in his body tighten, as if he's making an effort not to move.

"I said I didn't want a Vegas chapel. That I wanted a big wedding because I'd been working so hard with Nikki and saw everything she was choosing for her own wedding. I—I made you think I'd be cool with a wedding. With a marriage. But later when you started hinting that you were going to ask me, I backed away like a scared rabbit, and I—"

"Shhhh." His tone is gentle. Soothing. And he cups the back of my head and pulls me close. I'm enfolded in his arms, my face against his muscular chest, his body lean and hard against mine. And right then I feel as safe and as loved as I ever have.

"Do you think I don't understand?" he asks. "I do. You're frustrating as hell, Jamie, I'll grant you that. But I do get it. It was a big jump for you just getting involved. But we *are* involved now, kitten." Gently, he pushes back from me, breaking all contact, so that only our gazes are locked. "We've been involved now for years, and I—"

"I'm ready," I blurt.

For a split second, surprise floods his face, but it's quickly masked.

"I'm ready," I say again, because it feels good just to say it. "I was scared and...and now I don't even know what I was scared of. Not you, that's for sure. I could never be scared of you. Ryan, you've been perfect. So damn patient—I think I would have strangled me by now. But I'm finally—"

"You're ready," he says, sounding just a little confused. "You're really ready to be my wife."

"I—yeah. I really am."

"That," he says, "is exceptionally good to know."

He's smiling as he draws me to him, then kisses me, soft and sweet, before releasing me and stepping back.

For a moment, he just stands there looking at me in the ambient glow from the nearby restaurant. He looks as happy as I feel, and when he takes a single step backward, I'm certain that it's because he's about to drop to one knee, take my hand, and propose.

I hold my breath, waiting for him to just say the words so that I can throw my arms around him and squeal *yes, yes, a thousand times, yes!*

But he doesn't drop to one knee.

He doesn't take my hand.

Instead, he just nods thoughtfully. "Okay," he finally says.

"Okay?"

He smiles, wide and happy. "Okay," he repeats, and all I can do is laugh.

Sooner or later, he's going to ask me.

And this time, I know what my answer will be.

Chapter Four

"Wait," Ryan says.

We're in the parking structure, and he's latched the convertible's soft top back in place. I've got my hand on the door handle, and I'm about to open the door and get out. Instead, I pause and turn back to him, curious. I don't expect a proposal now—beach, yes; parking garage, no—so I really have no idea why we're waiting to go inside.

"Tilt your seat back and unbutton your jeans." His voice is firm, broaches no argument, and sends me from relaxed to wildly turned on in under a millisecond. That's probably what I love most about him—his ability to control me. A woman who is about as far from submissive as it's possible to get, and yet with Ryan, I always bend to his will. I'm his. Fully and completely, and he damn well knows it.

Just to yank his chain a bit, I consider pointing out that the seat doesn't recline very far in this two-seater gem, but instead I simply obey. I want what's coming, and if I hesitate or tease, he just might punish me. And not by a spanking, which we'd both enjoy far too much. But by denying me. And right now, I can't stand even the possibility.

Without any more hesitation, I press the lever to go back as far as I can, then I bite my lower lip as I very slowly undo the button fly on my Lucky jeans.

"All the way down to your ankles," he says. "Underwear, too. Then spread your knees as far as you can."

I hesitate, turning to him with wide eyes.

"Now," he says, and even though the parking area is well lit and the Thunderbird always attracts attention, I do as he says.

I do it because I understand why he's making me—because this is both punishment and reward.

He's punishing me for letting him doubt. For not fully committing to being his a long, long time ago.

And the punishment he's inflicting is the possibility of getting caught. Of knowing that I am completely at his mercy. That I have to do this because it turns him on. And because by being so open—so wild—I'm giving him power over me.

But the reward...well, the reward is the same damn thing—the possibility of getting caught. Of giving myself over exclusively to his whims. Because it excites me, too. And Ryan damn well knows it.

My jeans and underwear are around my ankles, and my knees are spread, one against the door, the other bumping against the casing that holds the gear shaft. I'm stretched wide, my legs forming a diamond. My skin is hot against the leather of the seat, and although he hasn't touched me, I'm already wet.

I shift my hips a little, then whisper, "Please."

But all Ryan does is smile and say, "Beautiful."

Since I'm desperate for more than words, I slide my hand down over my T-shirt, lower and lower until I reach the hem and my fingers graze the bare skin of my belly. He doesn't stop me, and so I turn my head to meet his eyes as I let my fingers roam even further south, tracing a straight path from my bellybutton to my clit.

His eyes are on mine, but his gaze flickers away as my fingers continue down. I'm waxed, and my mound is smooth and soft. Slowly, I go lower, shivering as I graze my clit, then sliding two fingers over my wet, slick labia.

I arch up as little shockwaves rock through me, the precursors to an orgasm, and that's when Ryan reaches out and closes his hand over my wrist. "No," he says firmly. "Hands above your head. Lock your wrists behind your headrest."

I consider protesting, but I know better. And so I do as he says.

"Good girl," he says as he tugs my shirt up above my breasts, then unfastens the front clasp of my bra. "Oh, kitten," he says, looking me up and down. "Do you know how hard it makes me, seeing how aroused you are? How tight your nipples are. How wet and slick your pussy is. Tell me," he demands. "Tell me you want me."

"You know I do," I say, arching my back a little in the hope that he'll touch me. "Please, Ryan. I want you."

"Mmm." The sound is deep in his throat, and it dies when he closes his mouth over my breast and sucks. I cry out, my body bucking and my hips gyrating. I am utterly under his spell, completely his. Anything he wants, I will give. Any demand, I will satisfy. All I want is him. His hands on me, his fingers inside me. And he takes pity on me, sliding his hand between my legs, then thrusting his fingers hard inside me.

I grind down, wanting to draw him in deeper, harder. "That's it, kitten," he murmurs. "Fuck my fingers. Take what you want."

I'm completely wild, completely turned on, and as his thumb teases my clit, I gyrate my hips, moving against his fingers that are so wonderfully deep inside me. I want to explode around him. I want to burst over the top—and I'm close. I'm so damn close.

My eyes are open, and I can see his mouth on my breast, and just that image alone takes me closer. But when a wash of headlights from a car entering the parking structure illuminates my skin, I know I should stop. Should slink down. But I don't. There's something enticing about the possibility that someone will see. That they'll glance in the car at just the right moment and see what we're doing.

Just the thought alone takes me that much closer, and when I hear the footsteps of whoever has just parked walking down the driveway behind my parking space, I actually whimper.

"Are you close, kitten?" Ryan asks. "Do you think he knows there's someone in this car? Do you think if you come he'll hear you cry out? Does that turn you on?" he asks, and then chuckles in response as my core tightens around his fingers. "Yeah, I think it does. Tell me you like it, kitten. Tell me you like being mine wherever I want you. Tell me I can fuck you anywhere. That you're mine in public and in private."

"I'm yours," I say, but those are the only words I can manage because I'm too close. Too near the edge. I don't really want to be caught—at least I don't think I do—but I can't deny that right now I'm more turned on than I can ever remember being, and part of the excitement is the edge that the danger brings to his touch.

And right now, he's about to push me over that edge.

I gulp in air, my body starting to quiver as the threads of a massive orgasm twist inside me, more and more and more. Closer and closer until I'm breathing hard and shallow, so close I know I'll die if I don't go over. And just when I'm there— when I'm only a hairbreadth from a full-on explosion, Ryan pulls his hand gently away, and what was reachable now seems like a faraway port in a storm.

"What—"

"You don't get to come, baby," he says in a low voice that keeps my senses humming and is laced with the promise of an even more amazing climax. "Not until I say you can. Are we clear?"

I nod.

"Are we clear?"

"Yes, sir."

He slides his hand back over my pussy, then thrusts inside me. "Lift your hips," he orders, and when I do, he slides a sex-slicked finger into my ass so that he's fucking me both ways, and the sensation is so incredible that I have to forcibly fight the urge to come right then.

But it's all over when he takes my breast in his mouth one more time and trails his teeth over my nipple. The explosion hits so fast and wild and huge that I can't hold it back, and I shatter completely under his vibrant, erotic ministrations.

When my body finishes shaking, I'm breathing hard and he's gently stroking my bare skin from cleavage to cunt. He's looking at me, too, his expression stern.

"Someone wasn't supposed to go there," he says.

"I didn't mean—"

He presses a finger to my lips to shut me up.

"I didn't ask for an explanation or an apology," he says. "But rules are rules, kitten. And I'm going to have to punish you when we get inside."

"Oh." My pussy clenches merely from the thought. "Um, how?"

"I think I may have to spank your ass until your cheeks are the perfect shade of pink."

I bite my lip, fighting a moan as my body warms simply from the thought.

"And then," he continues, "I'm going to fuck you so hard you scream my name."

"Oh," I say again. My mouth is dry and that's the only word I can manage. Frankly, I'm so turned on I'm amazed I can manage any words at all. "Okay."

"Pull up your jeans, baby."

I comply, my body shaking with desire. Ryan's always been able to arouse me with just a look, but right now it's beyond the pale. I'm so wet my thighs are slick, and the brush of my panties over my clit sends new shockwaves zipping through me.

"Oh no, baby," he says, obviously noticing. "You don't get to come again. Not just yet. Say 'yes, sir.'"

"Yes, sir."

"Tell me why."

"Because I'm yours," I say, then lick my dry lips. "And that means my orgasm belongs to you, too."

"Fuck yes, it does."

I glance down to where he's rubbing his very hard cock under his jeans, then I look up at him with a little smile. "I can take care of that for you, you know. I can take care of both of us, actually. My mouth. My hand..." I trail off in invitation.

"Careful, or you'll earn yourself more punishment," he says, and I only smile and sigh with pleasure. Because I know this man. And I know exactly what I'm in for once we get inside the apartment.

My body clenches in anticipation.

I know...and I really can't wait.

Chapter Five

"What's the matter, stud?" I ask, teasing. "Can't you get it in?"

"Watch it," Ryan says, finally sliding the key into the lock before he gives my ass a smack. "Unless you're looking for me to up your punishment?"

"Oh, how you dangle that carrot," I quip as he pushes the door open. I follow him in with my hands on his ass, and he whips me around as soon as we've cleared the threshold. Then he kicks the door shut with his foot and presses me hard against the wall, his hand cupping my crotch.

"Somebody is playing with fire."

I still have a hand on his ass, and I pull him harder to me. "Is that what I'm playing with?"

"I don't know. I—"

"Um, guys?"

I squeal from the unexpected voice, and Ryan leaps backward with more grace than I'd expect under the circumstances.

I shift sideways—and see the speaker sitting on my couch, her knees up under her chin, and a very uncomfortable expression on her face.

"Moira!" Ryan's voice is harsh, almost paternal. "What the hell are you doing here?"

Ryan's sister jumps up, her pretty, round face full of contrition. "I'm sorry. I'm so sorry!" She turns her wide brown eyes to me as she pushes a lock of curly dark hair out of her face. "I really needed to talk to Ryan, and I've lost my phone—I know, don't lecture—and so I thought I'd just come over. But you weren't here, and I remembered Ryan mentioning the brunch, and so I thought I'd just wait. I have the key you gave me from when I pet sat for Lady Meow-Meow, and I didn't think you'd mind."

"I don't mind," I say. "I was just surprised. And if you'd waited another second to say something, god only knows what you would have seen."

She glances toward Ryan, her lips pressed tight together. She looks like she's about to burst with laughter—and he turns a very charming shade of red.

Moira is one of the reasons Ryan settled in Los Angeles. He sold his security company to Stark International about the time she'd started at UCLA. He once told me that he moved here so that he could be closer and spoil her rotten, but the truth is he doesn't spoil her at all. Instead, he's been a father figure to her, and at twenty-two, Moira is capable and independent and smart. She's also become a good friend.

Someday, she'll be a good sister-in-law.

The thought makes me smile brighter. "We really don't mind," I say, since she still looks mortified. "But what's going on?"

"First, can you use that tracking thingie to find my phone?"

For a moment, Ryan looks about to lecture. Not surprising, since Moira is always losing her phone. But all he says is, "No problem." He starts to reach into his back pocket for his phone, but his hand stops as Moira continues talking.

"And second, I've been offered an internship this semester at Bradley-Costner."

I look at Ryan, who just shrugs.

"The advertising agency?" Moira says indignantly. "In Chicago? It's one of the biggest in the country, and this is a huge opportunity."

"How can you get an internship when you're already a

month into this semester?" Ryan asks.

"Well, there was some sort of mix-up. But if I can get someplace to live lined up this week and start work a week from tomorrow, then I can take the internship, get course credit, and drop my other classes without penalty."

"And so you're in Jamie's condo because why?"

"Waiting for you, dummy. There's no way I'll be able to find a place in time—not one that I can live in without Mom freaking out. I thought maybe you could help me?" She raises her shoulders, her expression pleading. And right then, I see how it was between them when they were kids. Him the older brother, almost like a father. And her, the charming and pretty little sister who had Ryan completely wrapped around his finger.

Honestly, it's completely adorable.

"When do you need to go?"

"Tomorrow," she says. "I need to be in Chicago to finalize all the paperwork and meet my boss by Tuesday morning. And then I figured I'd spend the rest of the day and Wednesday looking for a place and then Wednesday night, I'd head on to Boston to see Mom with you on Thursday. Please," she adds, making prayer hands. "You know you want to help. Otherwise who knows what kind of dive I might end up in. With some horrible, scalawag of a roommate."

"Scalawag?" Ryan repeats.

"Practically a pirate. Won't let me study. Will drag me to bars and seedy establishments. It'll be horrible. You just have to come."

He sags down onto the couch. "Well, that's where we have the problem. Because I'm trapped at work on Tuesday."

Her entire body sags. "Seriously? Maybe you could—"

"Can't do it, Polly," he says, which is his nickname for Moira. Apparently, she had a fascination with Ritz Crackers when she was a kid.

"But—okay, but...but Jamie could come with me." She finishes the sentence with a flourish, obviously having just concocted what she sees as a brilliant plan.

Personally, I'm not seeing it. "I don't know the first thing about helping you find a place to live in Chicago."

"But Ryan does. And he could set us up with an agent. Or maybe have his assistant line up a few places ahead of time. I mean, if Jamie gave the place a thumbs-up, that would be okay, right? You trust her, don't you?"

"He *so* doesn't trust me," I say. "With his little sister? Not even."

But Ryan is standing and nodding. "Of course I do, and I think it's a great idea. You are brilliant," he says, crossing to Moira and then kissing her cheek. "And you are sexy as hell," he continues, now looking at me. "And also damned responsible."

I make a noise in the back of my throat that might or might not be disbelief.

"Oh, gosh," Moira says. "I mean, if it's okay with you, Jamie. I just sort of blurted that out. I probably should have asked you first, not just—"

"It's fine," I assure her. "It'll be fun."

"And now that we've got that all straightened out, it's time for you to go." Ryan gives her a gentle nudge toward the door.

"My phone," she reminds him.

"Right." He pulls out his own phone, then curses when he looks at the screen. "Hang on," he says. "I missed a call." He lifts it to his ear and listens to a voicemail. When it's done, he's scowling.

"Well?" Moira presses before I can ask who the message is from. "Are you going to track it?"

"Hang on." He taps the screen, then raises a brow as he looks at her. "What's the name of that guy you're dating? The one who lives in Silver Lake?"

"Phil? I'm not dating him."

"Then I won't even ask how you managed to leave your phone at his house."

"Oh." Her cheeks turn pink. "Probably in the kitchen."

"Why don't you head on out and get it?"

"Right." She heads for the door, then turns back. "But—but what about the flight? Can we go on one of the Stark planes? And we need a hotel. And—"

"And I'll work it all out and text you," Ryan assures her. "It'll be commercial. The fleet's booked up this week. But you'll get there just fine, I promise. Now go before I rescind all offers of help."

"Aye-aye, Captain." She whips off a little salute to Ryan, then gives me a hug before bouncing out of the condo.

"You really don't mind?" Ryan asks me.

"It'll be fun." The more I think about it, the more I mean it. "We can mix up apartment hunting with shopping. Or just go out drinking. Who knows, maybe some cute guys will pick us up in her new neighborhood's bar."

"For the sake of those guys, I certainly hope not. No hands on my girl except mine." As if to illustrate the point, he slides his hands up and down my arms, and I sigh with a low, delicious pleasure, then grab his belt buckle to tug him closer.

"I think it's time for you to finish what you started, mister."

"Is that what you think?"

"Mmm hmm."

His lips brush mine in a gentle buss, but then he takes my lower lip with his teeth and tugs, and I feel it all the way to my core. "Maybe I should make you wait for it."

I'm sure that he's teasing, and so I'm laughing when I take a step back. But the laughter dies when I see his face. "The voicemail?" I ask.

"Believe me, the only one sorrier than you is me. This shouldn't take long, but I need to deal with it. And while I'm in the office I'll see about getting flights and hotel rooms for you two."

"You're a very cruel man, Ryan Hunter."

"Maybe I am. But I promise to be very good when I see you again."

Chapter Six

I don't know what crisis has exploded for Ryan, but I do know that it keeps him out all night. He's planning to be home by eleven, though, which is just enough time to drive me to LAX for my two o'clock flight with Moira to Chicago.

But a call at ten-thirty changes all that. I don't recognize the number, but I answer anyway. Usually, I ignore unfamiliar numbers, but today I'm afraid that Moira had to get a new phone—for all I know she lost it again—or that Ryan's calling from a landline at the on-site location he's visiting because the cell reception is crappy.

Whatever the reason, I answer—and am surprised as shit when the voice at the end of the unfamiliar number with a 310 area code is my mother.

"I'm in the airport," she says between saying hello and the time it takes me to ask why she's calling from an LA area code. "My phone ran out of juice, and they don't have plugs on the plane. Hundreds of thousands of dollars in technology, and they can't add a simple plug."

"They have plugs in first class," I say. "Next time upgrade. Why are you here? Can I talk to Dad?"

"I stopped at the first phone I saw after they let us off the plane. Can you come here? I could meet you. I think they'll let me out of security if I get another boarding pass."

"*Mom*," I say sharply. "Why are you at LAX at all?"

"I'm on a terribly long layover," she says. "I'm on my way

to Hawaii.”

"Really?” I'm excited for them. My parents never take a vacation. "Daddy must be thrilled.”

She makes a sniffing sound. "To tell the truth, sweetheart, I really don't know how your father is. We're separating.”

The words hit me like a punch in the face, and I actually stumble backward. "Separating? But—”

"I'm so sorry.” I hear my mom's wet sniffle. "Oh, there I go again.” She blows her nose loudly. "I didn't want to tell you this way,” she says. "I wanted to tell you in person.”

My mouth is hanging open, and I'm not sure if that's in shock or simply from the weight of all the questions I want to ask. But I don't ask a single one. Instead, I just say, "I have to catch a flight at two. I'll be there in an hour, and I'll meet you inside security.”

* * * *

One hour and twenty-two minutes later I've not only finished packing, but I've called Ryan and told him I'm taking myself to the airport to meet a friend who's on a long layover. I'm not entirely sure why I didn't tell him the truth—except, yes, I am sure. I'm not ready to talk to anyone except my mom about what she said. Because I still can't believe it's true. And the moment I say it out loud, it's like I've made it real.

At any rate, I've managed to get all the way from Studio City to LAX, park my car, make it through security, and sprint to the airline club where I'm meeting my mother. I don't actually belong to any of the clubs, but Nikki has a membership at all of them, and so I'd hit her up for a couple of passes. She'd texted them to me right away, and now I'm sitting at a table by the window with my mother across from me, looking out at the tarmac and assuring myself that this can't possibly be real.

Except it is. Painfully, awkwardly, horribly real. "But why?” I ask as the waitress brings me the pre-lunch glass of wine that I desperately need. I take a long sip. And then, since my mom still hasn't answered, I take another.

"Mom," I press. "What happened?"

Her mouth moves, as if she's not sure if she's supposed to be laughing or crying. "Life," she finally says. "Just...you know."

"No," I say. "I don't know." I hear panic rising in my voice. This makes no sense. My mother and father have been a fixture in my life. And, yes, I know that all parents are the center of their kids' lives, but these two have been like a stone edifice. A statue representing what complete love and devotion looks like. A love so intense and blinding that it actually scared me. First, because I was afraid I'd never find anything like it. And then later, because I was afraid that I'd get lost in it, sacrificing my own dreams and ambitions to the altar of couple-hood.

Is that what happened here? "Did you get bored? It's not too late to go to law school, Mom. I interviewed a guy a few weeks ago who started law school when he was fifty-five, and he—"

"No, that's not it." She presses her hand over mine, which is awkward because my hand is curled around the stem of my wine glass. And right now I really want to lift it and take another drink.

"Mom, please," I say as I watch tears well in her eyes. "Tell me what happened."

She pulls her hand back so that she can wipe the tears away. "I'm sorry. I didn't think I had any tears left to cry."

"You're staying with me," I say firmly. "I'll text Moira and tell her I have to cancel, and we'll go back to my place and eat chocolate cake and drink wine and watch every sappy romantic movie we can think of."

"No, sweetheart, you—"

"Mom, *yes*. You aren't putting me out or getting in the way or ruining my plans or any of those things."

Her smile is almost impish. "My sweet little girl. Do you

have any idea how much your father and I adore you?"

Her words startle me because all these years, their adoration was for each other, and I was left with sloppy seconds. She must see some of that on my face because she frowns, the expression deepening the furrows on her face, making her seem that much older and sadder. "Oh, baby. Your father and I—we were too damn selfish, weren't we?"

"No, you—"

"We were so wrapped up in each other." Her expression shifts to wistful, and despite everything she looks almost happy. Then it fades, and there's nothing left but the shadow of memories in her eyes.

"Mom?"

She shakes herself, and her familiar smile returns.

"Seriously, Mom, let's get out of here."

"Absolutely not. Melinda and Penny are already at the condo, and I have no intention of missing this trip."

I think back, trying to place the names. "The women you met at that Mahjong club you joined?"

"That's right. Melinda's husband died five year ago—not even sixty!—and Penny's husband left her, too. You could say we've bonded."

Too?

Penny's husband left her too?

"Wait—hold on, wait. You're saying Daddy left you? That's what started all this?"

Mom plasters on a smile, then nods. "Apparently his midlife crisis came a little late. I always thought once we passed fifty it was supposed to be smooth sailing down the other side of the mountain. But I was wrong." The smile turns rueful. "Like I was saying, maybe we were so wrapped up in each other we just burned out."

"Oh, God..." I lean back in my chair, my hand over my heart. My chest is tight and I have to remind myself to breathe, breathe, to just fucking *breathe*. "Is there—I mean, is he—oh, shit. Is he having an affair?"

I actually wince as I say the word. And, I notice, so does my mother.

But she doesn't answer. Instead, she bends down and picks up her bag. "I'm in a completely different terminal, sweetheart, so I'm going to go. I wanted to tell you in person so you could see that I'm okay."

I want to shout that she might be okay, but I'm not. How can my parents be separated? How can my dad be having an affair? *Is* he having an affair?

"You call and talk to your father, okay?" Her words are gentle. "No matter what, he loves you."

"Does he?" I say. "Maybe he just stopped. He stopped loving you, didn't he?"

She winces, and I feel eight years old. Not twenty-eight. "I'm sorry," I say. "I didn't mean that. I just—"

"I know, darling." She's at my side now, and I stand up, then lose myself in my mother's tight hug. "You go off and have fun in Chicago, okay? And you don't think about me or worry about me. I'm fine. We'll talk when I get back, okay?"

I nod, even though I don't want her to go.

I want to tell her about Ryan. About how he wants to get married. About how I'd been afraid, but then everything seemed so clear.

And about how now everything seems murky again. Like I'm in a dark room and everything is in shadows and I can no longer get my bearings. Everything seems surreal, like the whole world is just a trick of the light.

I feel as though I'm stumbling through the world, and maybe I am, because I sure as hell have no memory of getting to my gate. I'm just there, boarding pass in hand, when Moira jumps up from one of the uncomfortable plastic chairs and waves at me.

"Jamie! Over here!"

She waves me over, but I barely get two steps before she's bounced over to me and engulfed me in a hug. "I'm so excited!" she says, though she hardly needs words. Her body language says it all. She's so buzzed she's practically vibrating, and despite my own mood, I can't help but smile.

Apparently, my smile's a little weak, though, because she cocks her head and frowns as she peers at me. "Hey," she says. "You okay?"

There is no way—no way in hell—that I am letting my personal problems bring this girl down.

"I'm awesome," I say, and I will myself to mean it. "We're going to have a great time tonight. And you're going to kick serious ass tomorrow morning, and then we'll find you the most amazing apartment ever. Deal?"

She laughs and holds up a hand for a high-five. "Absolutely."

It's only a four-hour flight, but because of the time change, our plane doesn't land until after eight. By the time we get our bags and get from the airport to the Drake Hotel, it's almost ten and we decide to forego going out in favor of a drink at the bar.

"Only one, though," Moira says. "I have to be fresh tomorrow."

We go to our rooms only long enough to dump our luggage, then meet back in the bar. And by the time midnight rolls around, we've both finished two glasses of wine and are well on our way to finishing off the bottle.

"Should we get another bottle?" she asks, refilling her glass.

I pull the bottle away before she has the chance to pour too much. "Hold up there, cowboy. Weren't you the one who wanted only one glass?"

"Calms the nerves," she says. "I'll sleep better." She leans forward, her chin on her intertwined hands. "I'm kind of a nervous wreck."

"You totally have no reason to be. This is already yours, remember?"

Her mouth screws up in thought. "Nothing's ever set in stone."

I think of my parents' marriage and down the rest of my wine, then empty the bottle into my glass. "Good point. But I'm still cutting you off after that." I point to her partially filled glass.

She nods stoutly. "To the last drink," she says. "May it do the trick."

I clink my glass against hers. "And to your new internship."

"And to you and my brother," she adds before she takes a sip. She swallows and grins. "You know you guys are awesome together."

I sigh a little, because Ryan is half the country away, and tonight, I could really use his arms around me.

"Hey," Moira says, leaning forward with sleepy eyes. "You okay?"

"I just miss him." That's the truth. It's just not all of the truth.

We finish our drinks, sign the check to my room, and then head to our floor. "You're the best." She gives me a sloppy hug outside her room, then tells me she'll see me in the afternoon. "I'll text you after I get back from meeting with the team," she promises, then pouts. "It's unfair you get to sleep in."

"Aspirin and a full glass of water now," I say. "Trust me on that one."

She salutes, then shuts the door, and I'm left alone in the hallway in one of the loveliest hotels I've ever seen. I sigh, then head toward my room, wishing that Ryan was beside me and telling myself that I shouldn't call him the second I get to the room because I know he's working. He told me he was going to put in extra hours, so that he could ensure that he was free and clear on Thursday to spend time with his mother when she arrives in LA.

I don't want to be a needy, pain-in-the-ass girlfriend, and so I'll wait for him to text or call me. But that doesn't change the fact that I want him at my side.

I hesitate at my room and actually consider going down

for another drink. It's just going to be lonely in there. In the bar, at least I can be lonely surrounded by other people. But I don't want other people, either. Honestly, I'm not sure what I want. When I was with Moira, I didn't have to think about the bombshell my mom dropped on me. But now it's in my head—and I *so* don't want it to be.

"Fuck it," I mutter, then go inside. I'll read, fall asleep, and if I'm lucky I won't dream.

Because he's an amazing guy, Ryan booked a suite for both Moira and me, and when I walk in the living area, it glows with a dim orange light that's escaping from the partially closed bedroom. I drop my purse on the floor near my still-locked luggage and head that way, thankful that I'd left a lamp on so that I won't break my neck searching for a wall switch.

But when I reach the bedroom and pull the door fully open, I gasp and stand there in absolute shock. Because the light isn't coming from a lamp. It's coming from the room service style table set up at the foot of the bed. A table with three flickering candles, a bottle of champagne, and strawberries with chocolate fondue.

"Hello, kitten."

His voice comes from behind me, and I whirl around to find Ryan smiling at me. He's wearing jeans and a starched white button-down open at the collar. He's staring at me like I'm the only thing that matters in the world, and right in that moment I don't think I've ever been so happy to see anyone in my whole, entire life.

"Ryan," I say, but he just shakes his head and moves closer, then presses a finger against my mouth.

"No more talking," he says, reaching down for the hem of my T-shirt and pulling it over my head.

Already, I'm aroused. My inner thighs tingling. My cunt throbbing. My nipples hard and tight against the lace of my bra. I'm a little drunk, too. From alcohol. From happiness. From the touch of his finger against my bare skin.

Slowly, he traces the outline of my bra. Then he tugs the

cups down so that my breasts are both free and bound. I groan and bite my lower lip, because the sensation of cool air against my sensitive nipples is amazing. And all the more so when he urges me backward so that I'm pressed against the wall as he bends his head and then gently circles my nipple with the tip of his tongue before grazing the sensitive bud with his teeth.

I gasp, my fingers threading into his hair, the sensation driving me so crazy that I don't want him to stop. And when he *does* stop, I cry out, "*no*" in protest.

He presses a finger to my lips. "I thought I told you no talking. Baby, don't you know bad girls get punished?"

I swallow, my eyes wide. My skin tingles from the electricity that just those simple words send dancing over my body, and I feel the muscles of my sex clench greedily, longing for his fingers, his cock, his mouth.

But he gives me none of that. Instead, I see him slip his hand into his pocket, and when he takes it out, he has a simple chain with two plastic-tipped clamps on the end. Gently, he opens the clips and then fastens each end to my nipples.

My breath comes in stutters as my body adjusts to the pain as he tightens each clamp, sending a hot wire of pleasure shooting from my nipples down to my clit, now throbbing in time with the blood I feel pulsing through my breasts.

He takes a step back, his eyes going from my breasts to my face. Slowly, he smiles, his eyes lighting with humor and heat. He grasps the chain and gently tugs it, increasing the pressure on my breasts and pulling me to him. "Oh, yes, kitten," he says. "I do like that."

Slowly, he brushes his fingertips over the exposed tip of each nipple, and my body shakes unexpectedly as violent sparks cut through me and my cunt throbs in what feels like a series of small orgasms, winding me up and making me so wet and needy that if I were allowed to talk, I'd beg for him to please fuck me right then, right there.

"Go ahead, baby," he says, and though I don't realize at first what he's talking about, I realize that my hand has slipped under the waistband of the yoga pants I'd thrown on to run to the airport and meet my mother. "I want to watch you get off."

I don't hesitate. I want this too much. This wildness. This passion. I slip my fingers down over my clit and stroke myself as Ryan grabs the waistband and tugs the pants down. I'm wearing flats, and I kick them off, then scramble to get out of the pants as he tugs them over my feet.

He tosses them aside, then stands up, his hand going immediately to his zipper. He tugs it down and frees his cock, already rock hard. "Legs around my waist," he says, as his hands cup my ass and he lifts me.

I do what he says, letting him manipulate my body so that my legs are hooked around him and I'm held in place by that connection and the pressure of the wall against my back.

"Oh, baby," he says as his cock slides against my rear. "Lift up. Take all of me."

I put my hands on his shoulders and push myself up as he positions his cock. Then I lower myself, taking him in so slowly that his stuttering breath shakes my body, too, and his murmurs of, "oh, kitten, Christ, yes," make me that much wetter.

"I can't take it anymore," he says. "I have to feel you come."

He pumps into me, slamming us both against the hotel wall with such force I'm certain that my back will be bruised and the wall dented.

He's using both hands to keep my hips moving in time with his thrusts. But as I get closer—as my muscles start to contract around his cock—he uses one of his hands to tug on the chain connecting my nipples. A wild, crazed sensation cuts through me, and I explode, my body shattering in what has to be the most intense orgasm of my life.

"Hunter," I gasp as I cling, limp and sated, to him. "Oh, god, I love you."

He tilts my chin up, then kisses me sweetly. "Happy Valentine's Day," he murmurs. "And surprise."

Chapter Seven

"So this whole thing was a ruse?" I ask.

I'm naked on the bed, and Ryan is drawing designs with chocolate fondue on my body, then slowly licking it off. "Pretty much," he says, then sucks on a chocolate covered nipple. "I do love chocolate on Valentine's Day."

I moan and force myself to focus. "No working today? That was never a thing? Damien was in on it? Moira, too?"

"Mmm hmm." He drizzles champagne into my belly button, then sucks it out, making me squirm with pleasure.

"So Moira doesn't really have an internship?"

He looks up from where he's now trailing a chocolate covered strawberry straight down from my belly button. "No, that was real. That's why we set this whole thing up in Chicago."

"And your mom?"

"Still coming to LA on Thursday," he says, lightly tracing the chocolaty end of the strawberry along the folds of my labia.

"And—"

"Kitten? Shut up."

I lick my lips. "Yes, sir," I say.

He takes a bite of the strawberry he's been using to stroke me, his eyes hard on mine. "Delicious," he murmurs after he's swallowed. "Of course, now I'm thirsty."

He lifts the flute of champagne, but instead of drinking it, he drizzles it over my sex then takes a sip as the bubbles pop and fizz on my sensitive skin.

And then, while I'm still writhing from that sensation, he drinks the last from the flute, then closes his mouth over my cunt with the champagne still in it.

He teases and sucks and the feeling of the cool, tiny bubbles combined with his hot, hungry mouth is beyond amazing.

My clit is still sensitive, and before I know it, I'm flying again, this time thrust into heaven on a champagne high and Ryan's magic tongue.

"Good?" he asks, kissing his way back up my body once I've returned to sanity.

"Very," I say.

"Tired?"

I am, but no way am I admitting it. "Never," I say, and he smiles.

"Liar. But that's okay. I'm happy to wake you up. I have plans for you all night, you know. I intend to make the most of every hour of Valentine's Day."

"Do you?" I roll onto my side and snuggle close.

"Mmm," he says agreeably. "As a matter of fact, I have something for you I think will kick this day off right."

"Day?"

"It's well past midnight, kitten. A brand new day."

"Oh. Well, in that case, I can't wait to see what you have in mind." I prop myself up on my elbow and watch as he sits on the edge of the bed and tugs open the side table drawer. I start to joke that he got me a Gideon Bible, but even at this angle, I can see that whatever he's reaching for is important to him, so I bite my tongue. I remember our conversation on the beach, and a wave of emotion crashes over me with such power that I can't even identify it. Anticipation? Apprehension? Joy? Euphoria?

I don't know, and I only stay here frozen in this moment, as he pulls out a black velvet bag that's roughly the size of a book. He puts it on the bed, opens the drawstring, and begins to withdraw a familiar piece of pounded metal formed into a choker-style necklace.

"It's my necklace." It's a statement, but it comes out as a question. "It's the collar you bought me in Vegas."

"It is." He pulls it the rest of the way out. The pin that holds it closed is fastened in the back, so that the collar is a perfect circle. He's holding it at the front, his hand covering the small loop of silver, which is where a leash attaches.

I think about the night he bought that collar, not to mention all the other nights I wore it for him. Memories of being at his mercy. Of being pampered. Of losing myself in the sensual delight of giving myself over completely to him. To Hunter.

I swallow, my body on fire all over again, and not from champagne. "It's been months since I wore this," I say. "Why'd you bring it tonight?" I rise up onto my knees. I'm naked and I'm wet, and I lift my chin, giving him my neck. "What do you want me to do for you this Valentine's Day? Sir?" I add, playing the game.

"Close your eyes, kitten," he says, and I comply without question. I feel the brush of metal against my skin. The enticing click of the pin locking it on.

"I do like the way you look in it."

I lick my lips, but I keep my eyes closed. He hasn't told me I can open them. "You know I'm yours, sir. You don't need the collar. Whatever you want from me, it's yours. No questions asked."

"This is what I want," he says, and he takes my hand and lifts it to my neck, then presses my fingers to the leash-loop on the front. There's a thread tied there, and I trace it down until my fingers reach a ring—and my heart skips a beat.

"Go ahead," he says. "Tug it off and open your eyes."

It's tied with a loose knot that comes free when I give it a tug, and when I open my eyes I'm holding a stunning diamond solitaire.

I freeze—I just flat out freeze. And though it feels like an eternity, I'm sure it's only a heartbeat that passes before I gasp with surprise and lift my free hand so that my fingers are pressed against my lips. "Ryan."

He eases off the bed, then drops to one knee. Gently, he takes the ring off my palm, and holds it out to me. "I know you're mine, Jamie. Will you be my wife so that the world can know it, too?"

"I—" I make a small little gasping sound, then brush an errant tear away. My heart is screaming for me to cry out *yes, yes, a thousand times yes.*

But my head is whirring too fast. Images of my mother—so happily married and now separated—twirl in my head. Was all that happiness just an illusion? Was it never real? And if it was real—if she felt once how I feel about Ryan, then how could she and Daddy have ended up where they are now?

"Ryan, I—" I draw in a breath. "You planned all of this so you could propose?"

He doesn't speak, but the answer is clear enough on his face. Love and hope...and when I say nothing else, a hint of worry.

"It's just...it's all so much," I say. "So wonderful." I keep talking—words keep spilling from me. But not the word he wants to hear. Not the word I want to say. Because I *do* want to say it. I want to shout it. *Yes. Yes, Ryan, yes.*

And yet I don't. I stay silent, my words trapped behind a blanket of fear embroidered with the shock of my mother's words: *separation.*

"Jamie." He takes my hand, then rises so that he can sit on the bed next to me. Then—very slowly and very carefully—he says, "What's going on?"

"Nothing," I say automatically. I stand up, then go to the closet and slip on the hotel robe.

"Nothing," Ryan repeats, eyeing the robe up and down.

"I just—I just don't want to move too fast."

"Uh-huh." He pours himself a glass of champagne and

tosses it back before turning to face me straight on. "Did I imagine our conversation on the beach last Sunday? The one where you said you were ready?"

"No! Of course not!" Guilt washes over me, cold and gray. "But I get caught up in these warm, fuzzy feelings and I forget that—well, I forget that things can turn harsh."

"I see," he says, and right then it's his voice that sounds harsh.

"No," I say, blinking back tears. "You don't see at all. Because you don't know what happened. You don't know that things *did* turn. And now everything is all lopsided and wrong."

"Wrong," he repeats dully as he crosses to the window, then looks out at the darkened city. "So what are you saying? That you don't love me?"

"No!" I scramble off the bed and go to him. He's taken off his shirt, but he's still wearing his jeans. I stand behind him and press my face to his back, my hands on his hips. My fingers are in his belt loops, and for a moment I just hold on, looking at our reflection in the window. "I do love you," I promise. "It's just—oh, hell. I don't want to talk about this today. But my mom's in Hawaii."

He looks at me like I'm nuts.

"They're *separating*." My voice snaps like a rubber band.

"Oh, baby." I see his face visibly crumble. "I'm sorry. That's horrible."

I draw a deep breath, so relieved that he gets it. "Yes, exactly. So you see? It's not that I don't love you...I do. I just..."

"Just what?" he presses, and the relief I'd been feeling vanishes.

I bite my lower lip. "Ryan, they're... I mean, my mom and dad..."

"We're not your mother and father," he says. "And I understand that you're confused and angry at your parents, and maybe I should just back off. I don't know." He runs his fingers through his hair, then steps away, forcing me to let go of his jeans or follow like a leech. I let go.

He turns around to face me, the city to his back. "The thing is, I get you, Jamie. I really do. I get you. I've supported you. I love you. But most of all, I've waited for you."

"Ryan, I—"

He holds up a hand, cutting me off. "I've followed the path you laid because I didn't want to push you. But Jamie, I'm done. I'm officially pushing now." He drops to his knee again. "I want you to be my wife. Not my girlfriend. Not my roommate. My wife."

"Please. Just—" Panic rises in my voice, and I touch the collar. "You already know I'm yours."

"Do I? If you'll wear a collar, why won't you wear a ring? Are you only mine when we play? For the good times? For the rush?"

"No!" The protest whips out of me fast and immediate.

"I want a woman to stand by me through it all," he says. "When things get hard and messy. I want a family, Jamie, and all that goes with it." He draws a deep breath. "I came here today because I want that with you. And I thought you wanted it, too. And if that's not going to happen, I want to know. I want to know now, Jamie."

I swallow, my emotions boiling inside me. Anger, fear, frustration. But damned if I can tell if I'm frustrated with him or with me. I hear myself speaking even before I have time to plan out what I'm going to say. "You want to know?" I repeat. "So you can move on?"

He doesn't answer.

"Dammit, Ryan, you can't just dump this on me. Not after the day I've had. What I learned about my parents."

"I'm sorry about your mom and dad, I really am. But we're not them. Their problems aren't our problems." His eyes lock on mine. "Not unless you make them our problems."

"We should talk about this."

"We've talked this to death over the years, Jamie. I'm done talking. *Fuck.*" He grabs his shirt off the floor and pulls it back over his head.

"So that's it. You're just laying down an ultimatum?"

He pauses for a while, then he nods slowly. "I want to live my life with you, Jamie. I want to have kids with you. I want to grow old with you beside me. And I want you to be my wife. Not my girlfriend. Not my partner. My wife. If that makes me old-fashioned or a son-of-a-bitch, then I'm sorry. But that's what I want. Hell, it's what I need."

"We don't need a wedding to be happy," I say. I can hear the plea—and the panic—in my voice.

He just looks at me. Then I see his throat move as he swallows. When he speaks, his voice is even and calm, like we're talking about where to have dinner. "I'm going back to LA. If you change your mind, call me when you get back."

Oh, *hell no.*

"Screw that," I say, my temper flaring. I shake my head then start gathering my own clothes. "If anyone's leaving it's me." My bag's still packed. I can throw my leggings and T-shirt back on. I'll catch a cab and I'll get the fuck out of there.

So what if it's three o'clock in the morning? I figure there must be a six o'clock flight back to LA. I intend to be on it.

Yup. Unless Ryan stops me from walking out that door, I'm going to be on the first plane out of this city.

"So I'm going," I say, snagging my T-shirt on the slave collar as I pull it over my head. "You stay. Help Moira. Do whatever."

I wait, because of course he's going to tell me to stay, too. And we'll sleep and then talk about this like sane people in the morning. Because this is not the kind of thing that can break us up. We both want to be together, and that's the real bottom line. Isn't it?

But all he does is nod. And all he says is, "If that's the way you want it, then okay."

I gape at him. "That's all you have to say?"

"No." He takes a step toward me...and then continues past me into the bathroom. "Leave the collar on the bed."

Chapter Eight

When I wake up in my own bed, it's almost five o'clock on Wednesday. Which means I slept through Tuesday, Tuesday night, and much of Wednesday.

Obviously, I was exhausted after drinking with Moira Monday night, then surviving my drama with Ryan in the wee hours of the Tuesday that was also Valentine's Day, then waiting in the airport. And it's not like I got any sleep on the actual flight home. Damn turbulence.

I tell myself all of that, but it's not exhaustion that kept me sleeping for so long—it's the fact that I just wanted to curl up and escape.

Escape my thoughts. My fears.

Escape the fact that I hurt Ryan.

Escape the little bubble of anger that rises up every time I think about how he's laying this all on me. He's not even giving me time. I told him about the bombshell my parents dropped—and he knows how much the thought of marriage has always freaked me out—and even so he's demanding a decision right now. This very second. He's not even willing to just hang with the status quo for just a little bit longer.

But even that's not really what has me knotted up inside. Do I want more time? Sure. Do I wish that Ryan had cuddled me close instead of pushing me away? Absolutely. Am I totally annoyed with him because of that? Hell, yeah.

Mostly, though, I'm mad at myself.

And that's why I've been sleeping. So that I can escape that horrible, insecure part of me that refuses to say *yes* when I so desperately want to. Because I *do* want to. I want the happily ever after. I want it with Ryan.

But I don't know how to get there. How to get past this icy, debilitating fear. I want to—oh, dear god, I want to—but haven't got a clue how to push through, and every time I try, the cloying fear of failure and pain and loss pushes me back down all over again. I know it's stupid. I know it makes no sense. And know I should just be able to buck up and push past, and yet I can't.

I. Just. Can't.

And so I'd slept. I'd slid away into dreamland. Into a place where I didn't have to think or feel or do.

I'd run away—from Ryan, from myself.

And I hate myself for it.

Before I'd fallen into oblivion, I'd called Nikki. She hadn't answered, and I hadn't left a message. Now I check my phone, just in case she's called me back.

Or in case Ryan has called.

But there are no messages, and so I push myself upright in the bed, swing my feet off the side, and then just bend over and breathe.

I'm sitting like that—trying to decide whether I should get up to eat, go take a shower, or just fall back asleep in bed.

I'm still debating when my phone rings and I snatch it up, not even bothering to look at the screen. "Nikki?"

"Um, no. It's Moira."

"Oh." I cringe because until now I hadn't thought about how bitchy it was for me to just walk out. "Listen, I'm really sorry I bailed on you. I didn't—"

"It's okay," she says. "Really. I just—oh, hell, I just wanted to call and say that I don't know what exactly happened between you and Ryan, but you guys are great together, so I really hope you can fix it."

"Thanks," I say. "I—I hope so, too." That's probably the truest thing I've ever said, even though I don't know if we'll ever manage. Because fixing *it* means fixing *me*. And I don't know how to do that.

"And, well, I hope you're still coming to Mom's birthday dinner. I don't think Ryan's said anything to her about well, there being trouble between you guys. And I know she'd really love to see you, and—"

"I don't know, Moira," I say. "I just—"

She cuts me off with, "If you haven't talked to him since Chicago, you should."

"I haven't," I admit. "I've been—well, honestly, mostly I've been sleeping. Oh, Christ, Moira," I continue, because I'm full up and it's all just beating against me, and I have to get it out and tell someone. "I'm scared. And I don't know what to do. And I love him, but—"

"Then come," she says gently. "Come be part of the family."

"I'll think about it," I promise. And I will. I'll think about how awkward it will be. And I'll think about how much I want Ryan, a man who's given me an ultimatum that I can't meet. And I think that dinner will be torture, and how the hell can I do that to myself?

So I'll think about it...but I know damn well I won't go.

I'm still thinking about it Thursday morning as I sit in make-up before my morning slot at the anchor desk. And I'm still thinking about it after we go off the air and my producer tells me I look distracted.

"I've caught a bug," I lie. "It'll pass."

She frowns. "Look, just take Friday off. You're already off this weekend, anyway."

"You're sure?"

She nods. "Nothing personal, Jamie, but you look like hell. Go get some rest and come back next week healthy, okay?"

"Thanks," I say, not feeling the slightest bit guilty that I'm getting out of work by claiming I'm sick. I am, after all. I'm love sick...

I'm in my car heading home when Nikki calls me. "I saw that you'd called, but you didn't leave a message," she says after I've connected the call through the car's speaker system. "At first I thought maybe you accidentally called me, but I know you, James. And you haven't called or texted since I saw you on Sunday."

"Um, so?"

"So we haven't gone that long without talking to each other since high school. Something's wrong. Something you don't want to tell me. So tell."

I grimace. "Best friends can be a pain in the ass."

"You're welcome," she says, and for the first time in what feels like forever, I laugh.

I tell her to hold on while I get on the freeway, and then I tell her everything. Not just because she asked—and not just because I know she won't stop bugging me until I do—but because I have to talk it out with somebody.

"I can't go to Mrs. Hunter's birthday dinner," I say after I'm done laying it all out. "It's not fair to Ryan. And, well, I think it'll hurt too much to see him and then walk away again."

"Maybe that means you shouldn't walk away," she says gently.

"I'm not walking," I say stubbornly. "He's pushing."

She doesn't say anything. But that's okay. I speak fluent silence. So I understand exactly what she's saying.

Hell, I even know she's right.

I sigh. "It's just that I—"

I cut myself off. Just that I what? Don't really love him? That's not true at all. That I'm terrified? That's closer to the truth, but still not all of it. Because terrified of what? That he doesn't really love me?

No, I'm certain he does.

That he'll change his mind and stop pushing on the marriage front?

I frown, but that's not it either. It's close, though, because the one thing I am sure of is that my parents' separation is fueling this dark hole inside my gut. But knowing the cause doesn't mean I know the solution.

I tap the brake and exit the freeway, then tell Nikki that I have to go.

"Okay," she says. "But call me if you need to."

I assure her I will. Frankly, I hope that I do need to call her. At least that might mean that I need help moving forward. Right now, all I'm doing is floundering. And I can manage *that* all on my own.

When I get home, I glance at my phone to check any texts that came in while I was talking to Nikki. There's only one, and it's from Moira with the time and place of her mother's birthday dinner. *She says she can't wait to see you,* Moira has added, and I frown at those words, wondering if Mrs. Hunter really said that, or if Moira is doing her own brand of manipulation.

If it's really Mrs. Hunter—whom I adore—I hate to disappoint her. But at the same time, it's Ryan who I want to hear from. Ryan who I want telling me to come to the dinner.

I don't understand how two people who are so close can now be so far apart, and I can't deny that I'm afraid. Because what had started with the vibe of a fight now has the putrid scent of forever.

And forever's not a place I can go without Ryan at my side.

* * * *

Vault is a new Culver City restaurant that is the latest dining hotspot. The chef is supposedly a genius, and the building itself is fun because it used to be an old bank, and many of the bank-type fixtures still remain.

For example, customers can actually reserve the old vault and have a private dinner inside the room, now decorated with art that sports a monetary theme.

That's the room that the hostess leads me to when I ask for the Hunter party, and as I stand by the safe-style door and look at the huge steel cylinders that form the now-defunct locking mechanism, I can't help but think that if I go into that room, there will be no way out.

I wonder if that's a good thing or a bad thing.

My nerves are jangling, and I'm actually considering turning around and leaving when Ryan looks up from where he's standing by his mother. His eyes land on me, and I freeze—I just literally freeze in place. I try to read his expression, but there's nothing on his face. Not joy, not anger, not irritation, not indifference. It's as if I'm nothing, and my heart squeezes painfully at the realization that this is how it could be. That I could actually end up being nothing to this man.

Could I? Even if I walked away, could I ever truly not be a part of him? Because I know damn well that he will always be a part of me.

I'm still staring—my heart twisting at his nonchalance—when his lips curve into a slow smile and I see a spark of something I think is relief in his eyes.

His lips move, and I smile at the simple, silent greeting as he mouths a single word—*Hi.*

It's a truce, and I accept it gratefully. I enter the room, expecting him to come to me, but it's Moira who is at my side first, though Ryan joins a moment later and pulls my chair out for me.

It's just the four of us—me, Ryan, Moira, and Mrs. Hunter—so the meal is intimate. And though Ryan sits next to me, he never touches me during the meal. I'm not sure if Mrs. Hunter notices. Or at least I'm not sure until Ryan excuses himself for the men's room.

"Now then," she says, peering at me. "What's going on with you and my son? Are you two okay?"

Moira props her elbows on the table and leans forward.

And with both of them looking so earnestly at me, I can't

fight the tears that spring immediately to my eyes. "Honestly, Mrs. Hunter, I don't know."

"Angela," she says. "Haven't I told you to call me Angela?"

"Angela," I say gratefully, and a sweet warmth fills me simply from the thought that I'm part of this family, even if only for a moment.

"I won't ask why—he'll be back soon. But I will say that he loves you. Whatever else is going on between you, if you love him too, then you'll get back where you need to be. Trust me."

"Thanks." I catch Moira's eyes, and see that she's nodding, too. "Thanks to both of you."

Ryan steps back into the vault. "What are you thanking them for?"

"For letting me be here tonight," I say. "Thank you, too."

For just a second, I think he's going to not respond at all. Then he says, very softly, "Tonight, this is right where you belong."

I cling to those words, and for the rest of the meal and dessert, the conversation flows easier. And when Ryan's hand brushes mine as we both reach for the fudge sauce at the same time, I feel a shock of awareness cut through me. But when his eyes meet mine, all I feel is loss. Because tonight I'm going home alone, even though what I want is to be in Ryan's arms.

I know I could make that happen right now—all I have to do is say that I want to marry him. But when I let my thoughts linger on those simple words, my chest tightens, and suddenly I'm having a hard time breathing.

"Jamie?" Ryan's hand is on my shoulder. "Are you okay?"

I nod, wishing he wasn't touching me because it's so damn distracting—and at the same time wishing he'd never let go. "I'm fine," I lie. "My wine went down wrong."

I manage to keep a smile on my face for the short duration of the meal after that, then I stand and make my excuses, telling them I'm sure they want some family time alone.

I step out of the vault, and as I pause to make sure my phone is in my purse, Ryan joins me. "I'm glad you came," he says, taking my arm and pulling me aside. It's not an embrace, but I wish it were. I want him to hold me. To let me use his strength to get past this muck in my head.

I want to tell him as much, but somehow I can't find the words. Instead, I say, "I'm glad I came, too. Angela's great. Your whole family is," I add, thinking of Moira.

"I adore all of the women in my life," he says. "I'd do anything for them." He's looking at me as he says it, and my heart flutters in my chest. But I'm not sure if he's including me in that group, or if the hint of meaning I hear in his voice is nothing more than my imagination.

I shake my head as I frown, trying to clear my thoughts.

"You okay?"

"Fine," I say, though it's not true. Our rhythm is off, and it's scaring me. We've always been in sync, even before we were dating. And now—well, now it almost feels like he's deliberately keeping me off balance.

I want to get back to normal, and I don't know the path, and my lack of confidence is frustrating me.

"Are you heading home?" Ryan asks.

I shake my head. "Oh, I don't know. I haven't decided. You?"

"Moira and I are taking Mom back to the hotel."

I wait for him to invite me along, and when he doesn't, I say, "It'll be nice for you guys to have time to chat in the car. But she usually crashes early, doesn't she?"

"Usually. Why?"

"Oh. Um." I lick my lips. "Because I was wondering if you wanted to meet me somewhere. We could get a drink. We could talk."

"Talk," he repeats. He meets my eyes, and I see the question in them—have I changed my mind? Am I going to say yes?

I glance down at the floor.

"Talk," he repeats. "No, I'm sorry. I can't do that."

I look up, frustrated. "But, Ryan, I just—"

"I have plans. I'm going to Westerfield's."

"Oh." Westerfield's is one of the hottest clubs in town. It's also a Stark property, which means when Ryan goes he gets the full VIP treatment. Something that never fails to snag the attention of the female patrons. Most of whom are usually drunk. And wearing outfits that are barely big enough to keep a Barbie doll modest.

"Oh," I repeat.

I wait for him to suggest I join him there, but all he says is, "It really was great that you came." Then the bastard leans in and kisses my cheek. He kisses my *fucking cheek*.

And all that muck in my head starts churning, and all the anger and frustration I'm feeling toward myself comes spewing out—and, naturally, Ryan gets the brunt of my wrath.

"You're going clubbing?" I snap, pulling back to look at his face. "You're bussing my cheek? I thought I was the woman you loved? I thought you wanted to marry me. I hesitate for five seconds and suddenly you're over me?"

We're standing half-in and half-out of the vault. Inside that private room, Moira and Angela are trying very hard to pretend they aren't listening. In the main area, no one's pretending at all. They're gaping and enjoying the show.

"You are the woman I love, and I do want to marry you. But you've made it clear you don't want that. This is the world where we aren't together, Jamie. Did you think you could have it both ways?"

A ball of red rage bubbles inside me, and instead of spilling out of my mouth in a string of curses, it comes out in my hand—and I slap the shit out of him. "It's been two days. *Two days*. And I love you, you bastard. Think about *that* while you're playing these goddamn games."

And with that, I turn away from him, hike my purse strap more firmly on my shoulder, and storm out of the restaurant, a string of curses running like mutilated pearls through my head.

God*damn* him. Goddamn, goddamn, *goddamn* him.

And while I'm at it, goddamn me. Because maybe he is playing games. But maybe he's not.

Maybe this is all on me. Maybe I'm the one playing the game, and he's just changed the rules around to suit him.

I'm crying as I head home, but home isn't where I want to be. I pace. I drink. I pace some more.

But the wine doesn't taste good, and the back and forth motion across my floor isn't doing a damn thing for my temper.

Finally, I sit down at my kitchen table, press speed dial on my phone, and listen to the ringing at the other end of the line.

He answers on the third ring. "Jamie?"

I draw in a breath and realize tears are streaming down my face. "Daddy?"

"Oh, baby. I'm sorry—I should have called you, but I've been in such a state."

"A state," I repeat, my voice heavy with sarcasm. "What state are you in? Mom's in Hawaii."

He sighs. Loudly.

"Dammit, Daddy. What happened? Are you—I mean, are you having an affair?"

"No," he says, and I sag with relief. "Nothing really happened until your mother and I officially split."

Oh god.

"You're telling me there really is someone else?"

"Jamie, sweetie, I know this is hard—"

"Hard? You guys love each other. You practically worship each other. You—" I close my eyes and my mouth and try to regroup. "What the hell happened?"

"I don't know," he says, and though I don't like the answer, I think it's honest. There's a note of quiet resilience in his voice. As if he's come to terms with something unpleasant that he doesn't understand, but knows just simply *is*. "I think it's been happening for a long time. I think...well, I think somewhere along the way we took each other for granted. We assumed we knew the score, and we just stopped talking."

"But..." I trail off because I don't know what to say. I was expecting him to dodge my questions. Instead, he's given me honesty.

"So is this a forever thing? Do you think you'll get back together? Do you still love her?"

There's a pause, and then he says gently, "We'll just have to see, won't we? Wouldn't be worth living this life if I knew exactly where it was going, now would it?"

I blink and spill more fat tears down my cheeks. "That's what you used to say when I was a little girl."

"Meant it then. Mean it now."

I choke back another sob.

"Enough about all this. You tell me what's going on with you. How's Ryan?"

I squeeze my eyes tight in defense against another round of tears. "He's okay," I say. "We're both okay."

"Is that a fact?" I can hear the question in his voice.

"Honestly? No." I draw in a breath. "But we will be." I nod, those three simple words ringing in my mind—*We will be.* "Listen, Dad, I have to go. I'm—I'm sorry about you and Mom. I still can't really wrap my head around it."

"Sometimes I can't either. But no matter what happens, know that your mother and I both love you very much."

"I know," I whisper.

I hang up and sit there at the table for what feels like hours but is probably only minutes. My mind is churning with thoughts that are too hard to pin down because they're flickering too fast, more emotion than reason. More heart than mind.

I draw in a deep breath.

I can do this. I can overcome my fear.

I have to. Because the only thing I fear more than the great unknown of marriage is the certainty that I'll lose Ryan forever if I don't let him put a ring on my finger.

I attach my phone to a small tripod, set it to video mode,

and focus it on the couch.

Right now, I know exactly what I need to do.

Because smart or foolish, right or wrong, the bottom line is that I'll never really have a guarantee. I'll never be completely certain about anything I do with Ryan or with my life. All I can do is believe.

Right now, the thing I believe the most in is Ryan.

Chapter Nine

I consider texting him the video, but this is something I want to hand to him personally. And since I happen to know where to find him, I make the short drive over the hill to the club on Sunset Boulevard.

Fortunately, Damien added my name to the VIP list long ago, so I walk past the line and ease into the crowded venue. It's a Thursday, so the crowd is slightly less packed than it'll be come tomorrow, but that's not saying much.

I maneuver my way through the throng, trying to find Ryan in the sea of faces and the colored light reflected from the dance floor.

Since I'm having no luck, I head to the bar and signal for a drink. The bartender knows me and he nods in acknowledgement. While I wait, I turn and let my gaze roam the crowd one more time.

Nothing.

I'm just about to turn back to the bar to grab my Scotch when I see him. He's on the far side of the room, about to go up the stairs that lead to the manager's private office. And there's a very stacked blonde right beside him.

Seriously?

Two days since he gives me an ultimatum?

Less than two hours since he confirmed that he loves me

and wants to marry me, but says that it's all on me?

Not even a fucking week before he's hitting on a blonde in a tight knit dress?

Really? *Really?*

I gulp down my drink, leave a twenty on the bar, and push my way through the crowd. They're halfway up the stairs when I pound up behind them, then tug at Ryan's elbow.

"Jamie!"

"Do you want to explain yourself?"

For a second he looks confused, but when I shift my gaze quickly to blondie, he actually has the nerve to let his confusion morph into amusement. "No," he says. "I don't think I need to explain. I think the situation is perfectly clear."

"What happened to you love me? What happened to you want to put a ring on my finger? Are you planning to put a ring on her finger, too? Are you—"

"Wait," the girl says. "A ring? What?" She shifts her attention from me to Ryan. "Mr. Hunter, if you need some time to talk to—"

"Mr. Hunter?" I repeat. For a moment, I'm legitimately confused. But that confusion only lasts a second or two.

Soon enough, it fades away, replaced by something much, much worse: abject mortification.

"Oh," I say, trying on a smile. "Um, who are you?"

"Delaney Dawson," she says.

"Ms. Dawson is the new security specialist for Westerfield's," Ryan explains.

"Really?" I flash my most camera-ready smile. "Wow. Well. Congratulations. Everyone here is great. I'm sure you're going to really enjoy working with everyone at Westerfield's."

"I'm sure I will, too." Her smile is a little too bright, and I think she's trying very hard not to laugh.

"Delaney," Ryan says, "I realize this may be a little inconvenient, but do you think we could continue this briefing tomorrow? I need to speak with Ms. Archer alone."

"Not a problem," she says. She meets my eyes,

amusement twinkling in hers. "It was a pleasure meeting you."

"Yeah," I say, waving a limp hand after her as she heads back down the stairs. "A pleasure." I swallow. "Ryan, I'm so, so—"

"With me," he says, hurrying the rest of the way up to the management office. He pulls me inside, then slams the door behind us. And, I notice, he locks it.

"Ryan—"

But he shakes his head, silencing me, his expression like a wolf on the prowl. He takes a step toward me, and I take a step back, then another and another until I'm right in front of the wall of one-way glass that looks down on the dance floor below.

"You thought I was fucking Ms. Dawson?"

"Well, I...yeah."

He steps closer still, and now my back is to the glass and he's right in front of me, so close I can feel his heat and smell the scent of him, like earth and musk.

"If you're not with me, I'm a free man, Jamie. That means I can fuck whomever I want. Right?"

I swallow, but I don't speak. The thought of him with another woman is so horrible I can't quite wrap my mind around it, much less my words.

"But here's the thing, kitten. I don't want anybody else. Not to fuck. Not to hang out with in front of the television. You've destroyed me, Jamie." He reaches out, then cups my face in his palm. "You've destroyed me completely. And for that, I think you need to be punished."

"I—what?" My head is certain I've heard him wrong. But my body is right with the program. Heat has pooled between my thighs, and my nipples are tight against the lace bra I wore under the sheath dress I'd put on for dinner with Hunter's family.

"Turn around, baby," he orders. "Put your hands on the glass."

I do, and as I stare out at the dancers beyond, relief

explodes through me, along with a wild desire that is so palpable it makes my skin burn. Ryan pulls up my dress, then rips down my panties. "Is this what you want?" he asks. "For me to take you hard and fast? To punish you for thinking I could ever fuck another woman?"

"Yes," I say. "Oh, please, yes."

His hands slide over my ass, and he spreads me wide. "Christ, you're wet. I love it when you're wet for me."

His finger teases my core, slipping in and out of me as he lowers his zipper with his other hand. Then his hands are on my hips and his cock is at my center. He eases inside me, and I gasp, watching the dancers writhing beneath us as he fills me.

His fingers stroke my clit, expertly taking me to the edge. He keeps me there, teetering on the precipice as he pumps hard into me, lost in the rhythm of the music. Hard and fast with an increasing frenzy. Like an ancient dance. A mating ritual.

A claiming.

When he comes, he cries out my name, and I explode in his arms, my core milking his cock as he comes inside me, filling me completely.

When he cleans me up with a nearby tissue, he is tender and gentle and sweet. And then he picks me up and cradles me as he walks over to the sofa and carefully puts me down.

I'm sitting there, my skirt twisted awkwardly, my body still on fire, when he kneels in front of me. "I want you, Jamie. I want you to be my wife, but if you can't handle that, then okay. If this is what you want—the two of us together with no vows to bind us, then that's what you can have."

He draws a breath. "There's nothing I can deny you, Jamie. And god knows I won't force you to do something you don't want to do. I want you to be my wife, yes. But I'll take you any way I can have you."

I sit perfectly still for a moment. "Ryan," I finally say. "Are you sure?"

He drags his fingers through his hair, his shoulders rising

and falling as he sighs. "Sure? The only thing I'm sure about is you, kitten. Do you think these last few days have been easy on me? Do you think I've been playing a game?"

I start to open my mouth, but he presses his finger to my lips and shakes his head. "I want you as my wife, make no mistake. But I can't lose you. Seeing you at dinner with my mother and sister drove that home. And, yeah, you helped drive it home, too," he adds with a wry grin, as he lays his palm over his cheek where I slapped him.

"I'm sorry," I manage to say before he taps his finger on my lip in a not-so-subtle reminder that I'm not supposed to be speaking.

"Thanks for that. But the truth is, I'm sorry, too. I took the righteous high road. But when it comes right down to it, we both want the same thing. And it's no more fair of me to insist we get married than it is for you to insist we don't. And when I looked at it that way, I couldn't keep the fight up. Because you're the thing I'm most sure about in my life."

He brushes my cheek, and it's only then that I realize that I'm crying and that he's brushing away a tear.

"I can't lose you, kitten. And if I don't have a choice, then so be it."

I swallow because this is my out-clause. My Door Number Two.

This is the result I'd wanted, and Ryan has handed it to me as a gift.

I should sit back down and be done.

Except that's not what I want now.

I want everything.

And so instead of sitting, I go to my purse and grab my phone. I hand it to him. "It's a Valentine's Day present. I didn't give it to you on Tuesday because, well..."

"You're giving me your phone?"

I cock my head and raise an eyebrow as I go sit next to him. "A video," I say, finding the app. "I, um, originally planned to do this whole reporter theme, where I reported on all your virtues. But I didn't do that."

"No? Did you decide I don't have any virtues?"

"Haha. No, I just decided on a slightly different approach. So..." I wave my hand. "Go ahead. Watch it."

He looks at me, his mouth twitching with obvious amusement, then presses the icon to start the video playing. A split second later, there I am on the screen. Slightly off-center since I hadn't lined the camera up exactly where it should be.

"Um, yeah. So, this was supposed to be something different. A glowing report of all of your virtues. But, well, I guess it's a woman's prerogative to change her mind. And that's a good thing because I keep changing mine."

I clear my throat.

"Anyway, here's the thing..."

I trail off as I stand up, and for a moment, my head disappears off the top of the screen. Then it reappears when I lower to one knee. "I've been an idiot," I say. "A scared of my own shadow kind of idiot. But I'm not scared anymore."

I lick my lips and look straight into the camera. "I want to get married. I want to marry you in Vegas, where it all began. In a tacky little chapel without all the noise of a big wedding. I want to elope, Ryan. I want to go right now. This minute."

I exhale.

"I guess what I'm saying is this—Ryan Hunter, will you marry me?"

Then I smile, a little uncertain. "So, that's it. Um, okay..."

And I stand up and walk out of frame. A second later, the video ends.

"I didn't have time to edit it," I say, turning to see him staring at me with a look of wonder and adoration on his face. "I just shot it and then came to find you because I wanted you to see it, and—"

"Yes," he says.

My breath hitches. "You mean—"

"Yes. Yes, kitten, I'll marry you."

He pulls me onto his lap so that I am straddling him. I

laugh with delight, especially when I see that he looks as happy as I feel.

"Kiss me," I demand, and he doesn't hesitate. His mouth closes over mine, and he kisses me deeply. Passionately. The kind of kiss I feel all the way down to my toes and everywhere in between.

I shift forward so that my core rubs against his already hard cock. I'm breathing hard, and so is he. Slowly, he lifts my dress, then slides his finger between us. My panties are still by the window, and the sensation of his finger against my slick skin makes my body tingle.

"Make love to me," I say, looking into his eyes as I open his fly. His cock is hard and ready, and I lower myself onto him, claiming what is mine. "Make love to me slowly."

"Whatever you want," he murmurs, pressing soft kisses to the side of my mouth. "Anything you want. For tonight," he says. "And for the rest of our lives."

Chapter Ten

"You do realize that usually there aren't invited guests to an elopement." Nikki frowns thoughtfully at my hair as she talks, and I sit still in front of the mirror and remind myself that after as many pageants as she's been in, Nikki knows how to wield a curling iron.

"Is that even a word?"

"It is now," she says. "Okay, last strand. Now I just have to pin it up."

My hair is normally wavy, but it takes curl well, and now it's a mass of loose curls that frame my face. It's a little wild. Frankly, it reminds me of sex.

And I know that Ryan will like it just like this. "No," I say, holding up my hand. "Leave it. It's sexy."

She starts to protest—I know her so well I can just see it on her face—but then she just nods. "Let's get you dressed," she says as I take another sip of champagne.

"Pass me your phone," I demand, and she complies with a roll of her eyes, then laughs as I program in a personalized ringtone just for me—*Chapel of Love*, the classic by The Dixie Cups. "Now you'll never doubt it's me," I say, tipsy but oh, so happy.

Because this is my wedding day. And I'm already at the chapel.

I'd meant what I said in the video—I wanted a Vegas wedding at a tacky Vegas chapel.

And, yes, I'd wanted to elope. But I figure we make our own rules, and so there's nothing wrong with inviting Nikki and Damien, who flew in for the night from Austin. After all, she's my best friend in the world.

And Ryan can't get married without his sister and his mother. That just wouldn't be right. So they're already inside the chapel, waiting for me to change.

As for the rest of our friends and family...well, I'm all about the after-party.

"Okay, we're almost out of time," Nikki says. This little chapel only gives each bride thirty minutes to prep. "Let's get you zipped." I stand, and she reaches behind me and inches up the zipper. The dress is white and flowing, albeit simple. It's also just a little bit sexier than your traditional virginal white.

Ryan, I think, is going to love it.

"Am I ready?" I ask.

"I don't know," she answers. "Are you?"

I look at her and think of Ryan. "Yeah," I say as we head for the double wooden doors. "Let's go."

Tinny organ music starts the moment she pushes the door open for me. I step inside, take a deep breath, and look toward the front of the room.

Ryan is there, dressed in a dark blue suit and looking as happy as I've ever seen him.

I want to run to him, but I force myself to walk down the short aisle as Nikki moves off to the side to stand by Damien.

I continue, savoring this moment. The way Ryan looks at me. The smile on his face. The love in his eyes.

I reach his side and take his hand in mine. "Hey, kitten," he says, in a whisper meant only for me.

I hide my smile as I focus on the preacher, who goes through the familiar words that bind me to this man. *My* man.

Finally, he asks if I take him, Ryan, to be my husband. And that's when I say the words I've been waiting to voice.

The only words that matter.

"Yes," I say emphatically. "I do."

As the words leave my lips, I know with absolute certainly that this is the man I'm meant to spend my life with.

"I love you, Jamie Hunter," he says, once he's been given permission to kiss the bride. And as his lips claim mine in our first marital kiss, I close my eyes and let myself get swept away in warmth and love and joy.

We're starting a brand new adventure, I realize. And I can't wait to see where it takes us.

Also from 1001 Dark Nights and J. Kenner, discover Tame Me, Hold Me, Caress of Darkness, and Caress of Pleasure.

Sign up for the 1001 Dark Nights Newsletter
and be entered to win a Tiffany Lock necklace.

There's a contest every quarter!

Go to www.1001DarkNights.com to subscribe.

As a bonus, all subscribers will receive a free
1001 Dark Nights story
The First Night
by Lexi Blake and M.J. Rose

Turn the page for a full list of the
1001 Dark Nights fabulous novellas...

Discover 1001 Dark Nights Collection Four

Go to www.1001DarkNights.com for more information.

ROCK CHICK REAWAKENING by Kristen Ashley
A Rock Chick Novella

ADORING INK by Carrie Ann Ryan
A Montgomery Ink Novella

SWEET RIVALRY by K. Bromberg

SHADE'S LADY by Joanna Wylde
A Reapers MC Novella

RAZR by Larissa Ione
A Demonica Underworld Novella

ARRANGED by Lexi Blake
A Masters and Mercenaries Novella

TANGLED by Rebecca Zanetti
A Dark Protectors Novella

HOLD ME by J. Kenner
A Stark Ever After Novella

SOMEHOW, SOME WAY by Jennifer Probst
A Billionaire Builders Novella

TOO CLOSE TO CALL by Tessa Bailey
A Romancing the Clarksons Novella

HUNTED by Elisabeth Naughton
An Eternal Guardians Novella

EYES ON YOU by Laura Kaye
A Blasphemy Novella

BLADE by Alexandra Ivy/Laura Wright
A Bayou Heat Novella

DRAGON BURN by Donna Grant
A Dark Kings Novella

TRIPPED OUT by Lorelei James
A Blacktop Cowboys® Novella

STUD FINDER by Lauren Blakely

MIDNIGHT UNLEASHED by Lara Adrian
A Midnight Breed Novella

HALLOW BE THE HAUNT by Heather Graham
A Krewe of Hunters Novella

DIRTY FILTHY FIX by Laurelin Paige
A Fixed Novella

THE BED MATE by Kendall Ryan
A Room Mate Novella

NIGHT GAMES by CD Reiss
A Games Novella

NO RESERVATIONS by Kristen Proby
A Fusion Novella

DAWN OF SURRENDER by Liliana Hart
A MacKenzie Family Novella

Discover 1001 Dark Nights Collection One
Go to www.1001DarkNights.com for more information.

FOREVER WICKED by Shayla Black
CRIMSON TWILIGHT by Heather Graham
CAPTURED IN SURRENDER by Liliana Hart
SILENT BITE: A SCANGUARDS WEDDING by Tina
Folsom
DUNGEON GAMES by Lexi Blake
AZAGOTH by Larissa Ione
NEED YOU NOW by Lisa Renee Jones
SHOW ME, BABY by Cherise Sinclair
ROPED IN by Lorelei James
TEMPTED BY MIDNIGHT by Lara Adrian
THE FLAME by Christopher Rice
CARESS OF DARKNESS by Julie Kenner

Also from 1001 Dark Nights

TAME ME by J. Kenner

Discover 1001 Dark Nights Collection Two

Go to www.1001DarkNights.com for more information.

WICKED WOLF by Carrie Ann Ryan
WHEN IRISH EYES ARE HAUNTING by Heather Graham
EASY WITH YOU by Kristen Proby
MASTER OF FREEDOM by Cherise Sinclair
CARESS OF PLEASURE by Julie Kenner
ADORED by Lexi Blake
HADES by Larissa Ione
RAVAGED by Elisabeth Naughton
DREAM OF YOU by Jennifer L. Armentrout
STRIPPED DOWN by Lorelei James
RAGE/KILLIAN by Alexandra Ivy/Laura Wright
DRAGON KING by Donna Grant
PURE WICKED by Shayla Black
HARD AS STEEL by Laura Kaye
STROKE OF MIDNIGHT by Lara Adrian
ALL HALLOWS EVE by Heather Graham
KISS THE FLAME by Christopher Rice
DARING HER LOVE by Melissa Foster
TEASED by Rebecca Zanetti
THE PROMISE OF SURRENDER by Liliana Hart

Also from 1001 Dark Nights

THE SURRENDER GATE By Christopher Rice
SERVICING THE TARGET By Cherise Sinclair

Discover 1001 Dark Nights Collection Three

Go to www.1001DarkNights.com for more information.

About J. Kenner

J. Kenner (aka Julie Kenner) is the *New York Times*, *USA Today*, *Publishers Weekly*, *Wall Street Journal* and #1 International bestselling author of over seventy novels, novellas and short stories in a variety of genres.

JK has been praised by *Publishers Weekly* as an author with a "flair for dialogue and eccentric characterizations" and by *RT Bookclub* for having "cornered the market on sinfully attractive, dominant antiheroes and the women who swoon for them." A five-time finalist for Romance Writers of America's prestigious RITA award, JK took home the first RITA trophy awarded in the category of erotic romance in 2014 for her novel, *Claim Me* (book 2 of her Stark Trilogy).

In her previous career as an attorney, JK worked as a lawyer in Southern California and Texas. She currently lives in Central Texas, with her husband, two daughters, and two rather spastic cats.

Visit JK online at www.jkenner.com
Subscribe to JK's Newsletter
Text JKenner to 21000 to subscribe to JK's text alerts
Twitter: http://www.twitter.com/juliekenner
Instagram: http://www.instagram.com/juliekenner
Facebook Page: http://www.facebook.com/jkennerbooks
Facebook Fan Group:
https://www.facebook.com/groups/jkenner/

Discover More J. Kenner/Julie Kenner

Hold Me: A Stark Ever After Novella
By J. Kenner

Coming May 23, 2017

My life with Damien has never been fuller. Every day is a miracle, and every night I lose myself in the oasis of his arms.

But there are new challenges, too. Our families. Our careers. And new responsibilities that test us with unrelenting, unexpected trials.

I know we will survive—we have to. Because I cannot live without Damien by my side. But sometimes the darkness seems overwhelming, and I am terrified that the day will come when Damien cannot bring the light. And I will have to find the strength inside myself to find my way back into his arms.

* * * *

Tame Me: A Stark International Novella
By J. Kenner

Now Available

Aspiring actress Jamie Archer is on the run. From herself. From her wild child ways. From the screwed up life that she left behind in Los Angeles. And, most of all, from Ryan Hunter—the first man who has the potential to break through her defenses to see the dark fears and secrets she hides.

Stark International Security Chief Ryan Hunter knows only one thing for sure—he wants Jamie. Wants to hold her, make love to her, possess her, and claim her. Wants to do whatever it takes to make her his.

But after one night of bliss, Jamie bolts. And now it's up to Ryan to not only bring her back, but to convince her that she's running away from the best thing that ever happened to her—*him*.

* * * *

Caress of Darkness: A Dark Pleasures Novella
By Julie Kenner

Now Available

From the first moment I saw him, I knew that Rainer Engel was like no other man. Dangerously sexy and darkly mysterious, he both enticed me and terrified me.

I wanted to run—to fight against the heat that was building between us—but there was nowhere to go. I needed his help as much as I needed his touch. And so help me, I knew that I would do anything he asked in order to have both.

But even as our passion burned hot, the secrets in Raine's past reached out to destroy us … and we would both have to make the greatest sacrifice to find a love that would last forever.

Don't miss the next novellas in the Dark Pleasures series!

Find Me in Darkness, Find Me in Pleasure, Find Me in Passion, Caress of Pleasure…

* * * *

Storm, Texas.

Where passion runs hot, desire runs deep, and secrets have the power to destroy...

Nestled among rolling hills and painted with vibrant wildflowers, the bucolic town of Storm, Texas, seems like nothing short of perfection.

But there are secrets beneath the facade. Dark secrets. Powerful secrets. The kind that can destroy lives and tear families apart. The kind that can cut through a town like a tempest, leaving jealousy and destruction in its wake, along with shattered hopes and broken dreams. All it takes is one little thing to shatter that polish.

Rising Storm is a series conceived by Julie Kenner and Dee Davis to read like an on-going drama. Set in a small Texas town, *Rising Storm* is full of scandal, deceit, romance, passion, and secrets. Lots of secrets.

Go to http://risingstormbooks.com/ for more information.

Anchor Me
Stark Trilogy Book 4
By J. Kenner
Coming April 11, 2017

FROM NEW YORK TIMES AND #1 INTERNATIONAL BESTSELLING AUTHOR J. KENNER comes the highly anticipated fourth novel in the fast-paced series including Release Me, Claim Me, and Complete Me. This sexy, emotionally charged romance continues the story of Damien Stark, the powerful multimillionaire who's never had to take "no" for an answer, and his beloved wife Nikki Fairchild Stark, the Southern belle who only says "yes" on her own terms.

It's a new chapter in the life of Nikki and Damien Stark ...

Though shadows still haunt us, and ghosts from our past continue to threaten our happiness, my life with Damien is nothing short of perfection. He is my heart and my soul. My past and my future. He is the man who holds me together, and his love fuels my days and enchants my nights.

But when tragedy and challenge from both inside and outside the sanctity of our marriage begin to chip away at our happiness, I am forced to realize that even a perfect life can begin to crack. And if Damien and I are going to win this new battle, it will take all of our strength and love ...

* * * *

Chapter One

I look out the window at the beautifully manicured yards that line the wide street down which I am traveling in the sumptuous luxury of a classic Rolls Royce Phantom. A car so sleek and magical that I can't help but feel like a princess in a royal coach.

The road is shaded by parallel rows of massive oaks, their branches arcing over the street toward their counterparts to form a leafy canopy. Morning light fights its way between the leaves, creating golden beams in which dust sparkles and dances as if to a celebratory melody, adding to the illusion that we are moving through a fairy tale world.

All in all, it's a picture-perfect moment.

Except it's not. Not really. Or at least not to me.

Because as far as I'm concerned, this is no children's story.

This is Dallas. This is the neighborhood where I grew up. And that means that this isn't a fairy tale. It's a nightmare.

The branches aren't stunning—they're grasping. Reaching out to snare me. To hold me tight. To trap me.

The canopy doesn't mark a royal corridor leading to a castle. It leads to a cell. And it's not *The Dance of the Sugarplum Fairies* that fills the air. It is a requiem for the dead.

The world outside the car is lined with traps, and if I'm not careful, I'll be sucked in. Destroyed by the darkness that hides behind the false facades of these stately houses. Surrounded not by a bright children's tale, but by a horror movie, lured in by the promise of beauty and then trapped forever and slowly destroyed, ripped to pieces by the monsters in the dark.

Breathe, I tell myself. *You can do this. You just have to remember to breathe.*

"Nikki. *Nikki.*"

Damien's voice startles me back to reality, and I jerk upright, calling upon perfect posture to ward off the ghosts of my memories.

His tone is soft, profoundly gentle, but when I glance toward him, I see that his eyes have dipped to my lap.

For a moment, I'm confused, then I realize that I've inched up my skirt, and my fingertip is slowly tracing the violent scar that mars my inner thigh. A souvenir of the deep, ugly wound that I inflicted upon myself a decade ago when I was desperate to find a way to release all the pent-up anger and fear and pain that swirled inside me like a phalanx of demons.

I yank my hand away, then turn to look out the window, feeling oddly, stupidly ashamed.

He says nothing, but the car moves to the curb and then rolls to a stop. A moment later, Damien's fingers twine with mine. I hold tight, drawing strength, and when I shift to look at him more directly, I see worry etched in the hard angles of that perfect face and reflected in those exceptional, dual-colored eyes.

Worry, yes. But it is the rest of what I see that takes my breath away. Understanding. Support. Respect.

Most of all, I see a love so fierce it has the power to melt me, and I revel in its power to soothe.

He is the biggest miracle of my life, and there are moments when I still can't believe that he is mine.

Damien Stark. My husband, my lover, my best friend. A man who commands an empire with a firm, controlling hand. Who takes orders from no one, and yet today is playing chauffeur so that he can stand beside me while I confront my past.

For a moment, I simply soak him in. His strength, apparent in both his commanding manner and the long, lean lines of his athletic body. His support reflected in those eyes that see me so intimately. That have, over the years, learned all my secrets.

Damien knows every scar on my body, as well as the story behind each. He knows the depth of my pain, and he knows how far I have come. How far his love has helped me come.

Most of all, he knows what it has cost me to return to Texas. To drive these streets. To look out at this neighborhood so full of pain and dark memories.

With a small shiver, I pull my hand free so that I can hug myself.

"Oh, baby." The concern in his voice is so thick I can almost grab hold of it. "Nikki, you don't have to do this."

"I do." My words sound ragged, my throat too clogged with unshed tears to speak normally.

"Sweetheart—"

I wait, expecting him to continue, but he's gone silent. I see the tension on his face, as if he's uncertain what to say or how to say it—but Damien Stark is never unsure. Not about business. Not about himself. Not about me.

And yet right now he's hesitating. Treating me like I'm something fragile and breakable.

An unexpected shock of anger cuts through me. Not at him, but at myself. Because, dammit, he's right. In this moment, I'm as fragile as I've ever been, and that's not a pleasant realization. I've fought so hard to be strong, and with Damien at my side, I've succeeded.

But here I am, all my hard work shot to hell simply because I've returned to my hometown.

"You think coming here is a mistake." I snap the words at him, but it's not Damien I'm irritated with, it's me.

"No." He doesn't hesitate, and I take some comfort in the speed and certainty of his response. "But I do wonder if now is the right time. Maybe tomorrow would be better. After your meetings."

We've come to Texas not so that I can torture myself by driving through my old neighborhood to visit my estranged mother, but because I'm vying to land a contract with one of the top web development companies in the country. It's looking to roll out a series of apps, both for internal use among its employees and externally for its clients.

I'd submitted a proposal and am now one of only five companies invited to come to Dallas to pitch, and my little company is by far the smallest and the newest. I suspect, of course, that part of the reason I got the invitation is because I'm married to Damien Stark, and because my company has already licensed software to Stark International.

A year ago, that would have bothered me.

Not anymore. I'm damn good at what I do, and if my last

name gets me a foot in the door, then so be it. I don't care how the opportunity comes because I know that my work is top-notch, and if I get the job, it will be on the merits of my proposal and my presentation.

It's a huge opportunity, and one I don't want to screw up. Especially since my goal for the next eighteen months is to build up my receivables, hire five employees, and take over the full floor of the building that houses my office condo.

I'd worked on my business plan for months, and was a complete nervous wreck the night I handed it to my master of the universe, brilliantly entrepreneurial husband for review. When he'd given it the Damien Stark seal of approval, I practically collapsed with relief. My plan to grow my business doesn't hinge on me getting this job—but landing it will mean I can bump all my target dates up by six months. More importantly, winning this contract will put my business firmly on the competitive map.

My shoulders sag a bit as I meet his eyes. "You're afraid that seeing Mother is going to throw me off my game. That I'll flub tomorrow's meetings and hurt my chances of landing the contract."

"I want you at your best."

"I know you do," I say sincerely, because Damien has never been anything but supportive. "Don't you get it? That's why we're here. It's like a preemptive strike."

His brow furrows, but before he can ask what I mean, I rush to explain. "Just being in Dallas messes with my head— we both know that. She haunts this town. And having you here with me now makes it so much better. But you can't always be with me, and before I make my pitch, I need to be certain that I can travel back and forth between LA and Dallas without being afraid I'll see her around every corner."

The pathetic truth is that lately I've been seeing my mother around all sorts of corners. I've imagined seeing her in Beverly Hills shopping centers. On Malibu beaches. In crowded streets. At charity events. I have no idea why this woman I've worked so hard to block from my mind is suddenly at the forefront of my imagination, but she is.

And I really don't want her there.

I draw a breath, hoping he understands. "I need to lay all these demons to rest and just do my work. Please," I add, my voice imploring. "Please tell me you understand."

"I do," he says, then takes my hand and gently kisses my fingertips. As he does, his phone rings. It's sitting on the console, and I can see that the caller is his attorney, Charles Maynard.

"Don't you need to take it?" I ask, as he scowls, then declines the call.

"It can wait."

There's a hard edge to his voice, and I wonder what he's not telling me. Not that Damien keeps me informed about every aspect of his business—considering he pretty much owns and operates the entire planet and a few distant solar systems, that would require far too many updates—but he does tend to keep me in the loop on things that are troubling him.

I frown. It's clear that he's not telling me because I already have plenty on my mind. And while I appreciate the sentiment, I don't like that—once again—my mother has come between my husband and me.

"You should call him back," I say. "If he's calling on a Sunday, it must be important . . ."

I let the words trail away, hoping to give him an opening, but all he does is shake his head. "Don't worry about it," he says, even as his phone signals an incoming text.

He snatches it up, but not before I see Charles's name flash on the lock screen again, this time with a single word: *Urgent*.

Damien meets my eyes, and for just a moment his frustration is almost comical. Then he snatches up the phone and hits the button to call Charles. A second later, he's saying, "Dammit, I told you I can't be bothered with this right now."

He listens to the response, the furrows in his brow

growing deeper. Finally, he sighs, looking more frustrated than I've seen him in a long time.

Cold foreboding washes over me. Damien isn't the kind of man who gets frustrated over business deals. On the contrary, the harder and more challenging the deal, the more he thrives.

Which means this is personal.

"I hear you, Charles, but I'm not paying you for your advice on this. I'm paying you for those resources you're so keen on touting. So use them, dammit. Pull out all the stops and get me some answers by the time I'm back in LA. Fine," he adds after another pause. "Call me if you have something definitive. Otherwise I'll see you in a couple of days."

He ends the call and slams the phone back down. I open my mouth, intending to ask him what's happening, but before I get the chance, he pulls me roughly to him and closes his mouth over mine. The kiss is hard, brutal, and I slide closer, losing myself in the wildness. And for this moment at least, I forget my apprehension and his problems. There is nothing but us, our passion a raging blaze that clears away the debris of our lives, stripping us to the bone until there is nothing left but the two of us.

I'm breathing hard when we break apart, my lips bruised and tingling, my body burning. I want to turn around and go back to the hotel. I want to strip off my clothes and feel his hands on me, his cock inside me. I want it wild. Raw. Pain and pleasure so intense I get lost in them. Passion so violent it breaks me. And Damien—always Damien—right there to put me back together again.

On behalf of 1001 Dark Nights,

Liz Berry and M.J. Rose would like to thank ~

Steve Berry
Doug Scofield
Kim Guidroz
Jillian Stein
InkSlinger PR
Dan Slater
Asha Hossain
Chris Graham
Pamela Jamison
Fedora Chen
Jessica Johns
Dylan Stockton
Richard Blake
BookTrib After Dark
and Simon Lipskar

Made in the USA
San Bernardino, CA
01 February 2020

63888554R00068